THE
IRON
STAIRCASE

THE IRON STAIRCASE

Georges Simenon

Translated from the French by Eileen Ellenbogen

A HARVEST/HBJ BOOK
A HELEN AND KURT WOLFF BOOK
HARCOURT BRACE JOVANOVICH, PUBLISHERS
NEW YORK AND LONDON

Library of Congress Cataloging in Publication Data

Simenon, Georges, 1903-
The iron staircase.
(A Harvest/HBJ book)
Translation of L'escalier de fer.
"A Helen and Kurt Wolff book."
I. Title.
[PQ2637.I53E713   1981]   843'.912   80-25624
ISBN 0-15-645484-X

First Harvest/HBJ edition 1981

A B C D E F G H I J

THE
IRON
STAIRCASE

The first note was written in pencil, on a sheet of writing paper the size of a postcard. He did not think it necessary to put the date in full.

"*Tuesday: Attack at 2:50. Duration, 35 minutes. Colic. Ate mashed potatoes at lunch.*"

After the word "lunch," he drew a minus sign and circled it. This meant that his wife had not eaten any of the mashed potatoes. For years she had avoided starch, for fear of putting on weight.

Had Fernande, the new maid, had mashed potatoes? As she ate in the kitchen, he did not know and dared not ask her. Anyway, it was not in itself of great significance.

It was growing dark. The room, on the mezzanine level, was low-ceilinged, and the lights had to be turned on earlier than in the rest of the house.

He heard the click of the cash register at the foot of the iron staircase, and his wife's voice speaking to a customer:

"We've had no summer to speak of, but it feels like winter already."

3

October was not far off. As always at this time of year, Boulevard de Clichy and Boulevard Rochechouart were overrun with fairground booths, shooting galleries, and merry-go-rounds.

His wife saw the customer to the door, and he heard the tinkle of the bell. She would walk back to the till, he thought, and maybe she would look toward the stairs and call up, as she had already done several times during the afternoon:

"Feeling all right?"

Each time he had answered, "Yes, fine," even in the throes of his attack, as he clenched his hand to his chest in agony and stared at the wall.

Invariably she added, "Do you need anything?"

"No," and after a pause, "thank you."

She believed he was reading. That was what he normally did every day, from morning to night, even at mealtimes, during his annual attack of the flu. As far back as he could remember, he had had the flu once each winter, fairly early in the season. The symptoms varied. Sometimes he would get tonsillitis with a very high temperature, sometimes a head cold with aches and pains all over.

In the old days, his mother fed him at such times on egg flips, which he sipped slowly, without looking up from his magazine.

Louise did not give him egg flips, but plied him with the same lukewarm lemonade that he had been given as a child. The taste had not changed; neither had the peculiar, anemic yellow of lemons floating in a glass jug. She had started a new tradition: eucalyptus leaves soaking in water over a very old copper heater, used only for this purpose, with a little wavering flame like a vestal lamp.

He heard her footsteps below. She did not stop at the till,

but went to the back of the shop, doubtless on the way into Monsieur Théo's glass-walled workshop, which he never left before six.

It was five o'clock. The lights were on in the shop. He was made aware of this by the luminous halo emanating from the iron staircase. Outside, too, the façade of the bumper-car ring, just opposite the house, with all its lights switched on, shone with dazzling brilliance in the twilight, and from the red-curtained booth of a fortuneteller he could hear the sound of a buzzer that reminded him—God knows why—of the little vibrating wheel used by dentists.

Louise was no longer moving around. She was either busy tidying the counter at the back of the shop, where the smaller items of office equipment were kept, or in the printing office talking to old Théo.

It irked him not to know precisely where she was, and he wrote very quickly, like a schoolboy afraid of being found out:

"Same thing last Tuesday about 3:30. Mashed potatoes then as well."

He listened more attentively, till he could hear the beating of his heart and the muffled sound of the printing press in Monsieur Théo's cage. Then he glanced furtively around the room.

Between the two windows there was a bookcase. On the lower shelf were an illustrated edition of Balzac and the complete works of Alexandre Dumas, with yellowing pages embellished with etchings. These had belonged to his wife's father.

As they did not quite fill the shelf, there were also three or four prizes that Louise had won at her convent school, put there because they were of about the right size. These included a history of Lourdes and J. H. Fabre's *Social Life in the Insect World,* next to an album of erotic engravings by Rops.

Standing on the rug, he took out the Fabre, which he could not remember ever having opened himself or seen his wife open, and slipped the sheet of writing paper into it.

He was still there in his bare feet, his pajamas damp with sweat, when he was startled by Louise's voice:

"Are you out of bed?"

She was standing at the foot of the stairs. Though they could not see each other, they were very close together, for the iron staircase came up into a corner of the room, between the doors to the bathroom and dining room.

Taken by surprise, he just stopped himself from blurting out a foolish lie. As he made no reply, she persisted:

"What are you doing?"

"I'm getting another book."

Well, he would have to take one out now. She knew what he had been reading at lunchtime. It was a Balzac. Every year during his bout of the flu, he reread a few Balzac or Dumas novels.

"Couldn't you have called me?"

He heard her coming up the first few steps. The iron treads rang under her feet. There were only seven or eight more to climb, and her head would be level with the floor.

"Have you finished *Cousin Pons?*"

He could not say yes. She would know that it was not true. Now she could see him, and he was afraid that she would notice his guilty expression. He had never been able to look anything but guilty when he told a lie, or even when he was merely holding something back.

Careful not to look toward her, he said:

6

"I felt like a change."

Though he kept his eyes on the bookcase, he could see a blurred outline of his wife's head in one corner of his field of vision, and, in the half-light, her hair seemed blacker and more lustrous, her face almost luminously white.

"What did you take?"

It was a perfectly natural question. They always told each other what they were reading, and talked about it. All the same, he reddened, because he did not know, and because he felt her looking all around the room with the calm deliberation with which she did everything.

He squinted at the book in his hand, trying to read the title without lowering his head. At this moment, he was saved from further embarrassment by the ringing of the front door bell.

His wife began backing down the stairs.

"Go back to bed," she said. "I'll get Fernande to make you a pitcher of lemonade."

The shop was connected not only to the bedroom, by the iron staircase, but also to the kitchen, by a speaking tube next to the till. Like the words "Evariste Birard, Printer and Stationer" painted on the shop front in lettering more appropriate to some public building, the staircase and speaking tube were relics from the days of Louise's father. In those days the entrance to the apartment was via the main staircase, but this involved going out into the street and under the archway.

The childbirths of Evariste Birard's wife had not been easy. After each one, she had spent months in bed and, later, sitting up in the room, and it was then that the spiral staircase had been installed.

Oddly enough, this staircase proved even more useful when Birard was stricken with tuberculosis and confined to the bedroom, while his wife took over in the shop. It was she who thought of having the speaking tube put in, so that she could give orders to the maid without having to use the stairs.

The staircase had been invaluable on another occasion, besides Etienne's annual attack of the flu, but he preferred not to dwell on that. He had thought about it all too often lately, in spite of determined efforts to put it out of his mind.

The absurd thing was that he would have been hard put to say how the idea ever entered his mind. He blushed faintly at the few words he had just scribbled on the sheet of writing paper. If his wife happened to see them, what would she make of them? What explanation could he give?

From time to time he had caught Louise looking at him with a hint of uneasiness, as though she sensed some change in him. This was open to two different interpretations.

Besides, the notes had not been his idea, but that of the doctor on Avenue des Ternes, whose name he did not even know.

He put off the moment when he must stretch out his hand to switch on the bedside lamp. Often at night when they went to bed, they left the drapes undrawn and the lights switched off, especially at the time of the fair, when they could see all the side-show illuminations stirring in the sky, through the muslin curtains. Some of them were reflected on the walls, on the ceiling, lighting up the face of one or the other for a brief moment, or gliding across Louise's white body as she massaged her breasts after taking off her girdle.

Even when there was no fair, every night the raspberry-red glow of a late cabaret at the corner of Rue Blanche, a few steps from the house, permeated the apartment from nine o'clock on.

"Aren't you going to switch on the light?"

"Not just yet."

She always knew as well as he did what this meant. Louise stretched herself out on the bed without drawing up the covers. They could both hear the barely muffled sounds of the street outside. It was almost as though they were on the very fringe of the crowd, and, from time to time, suddenly, an unknown voice, distinguishable words rising above the general hubbub, would intrude on their intimacy.

For several years past, on a plot separated from the bumper cars only by the narrow booth of the fortuneteller, there had been a new side show. It fascinated them. Its swings were not such as children play on, but gigantic constructions enclosed for safety in a cage of wire netting. There were two of them, side by side. A single lamp, the most powerful and blinding in the fairground, illuminated them from below like a searchlight. Generally, two men standing face to face were needed to make the complete circuit. At the start, the swings were horizontal, then gradually, with each movement of the swinging man, they would tilt more and more, forcing his feet up and his head down. Finally, they would reach the vertical position, with the man's body straight and rigid, head down and feet up. At this point it always seemed as though the swings were arrested in flight, and that there was a second's pause before they began their descent.

Etienne recalled several mild evenings when they had stood at the window with their elbows on the sill, watching with fascinated absorption the curly-haired athlete in the white sweater who was the only one able to manage the swings without help, and who would often perform the feat over and over again without a pause, to attract customers. Once Louise had murmured, "He's like an archangel." At the time he had not been particularly struck by the remark.

She was talking downstairs. He could not hear what she was saying, because she was again standing near the door. Mechanically, he waited for the sound of the bell signaling the customer's departure.

It would not do for her to find him in the dark. He switched on the light and rested the book on his raised knees. She walked back to the till, and whistled into the speaking tube to attract Fernande's attention. Then Etienne could hear Fernande's muffled voice from the kitchen.

"Take some lemonade to monsieur."

"Yes, madame."

"Have you got enough lemons?"

"Yes, madame."

This was the time for Louise to begin clearing up the shop before going out to lower the steel shutters. Soon Jean-Louis, the delivery boy, would come back from his rounds and park the carrier-tricycle in the shed at the end of the yard. Etienne had not heard the voice of Monsieur Charles, the stockman, that afternoon. Perhaps he, too, had the flu. Etienne could not remember having heard him during the morning, either. His wife had said nothing to him. Usually, they told each other everything. She must have forgotten. They had lived together for so long that they sometimes felt there was no need to speak.

Was it he who had been the first to keep things back? He was not sure, but he might remember later, and if so, he would make a note of it along with everything else.

The strangest thing was that he simply could not recall when he had begun to feel ill, though this might be because it had not happened all at once. It had come on gradually. Still, he was at least sure that it was a few days after the New Year that he had decided to give up smoking. Before that, he had smoked two packs of cigarettes a day.

Had he been feeling a bit run down? It was quite likely. He was past forty, more often out of breath nowadays, going upstairs, for instance, or running for a bus.

Once or twice before, he had remarked, not very seriously, "One of these days, I'm going to give up cigarettes."

Louise had looked at him without surprise. Did she even then have that look that he found so disturbing? He could not say. It was not that she seemed anxious, but, rather, as though she were watching him from the outside, making a mental note of things of which he himself was unaware.

He had not been ill at that time. According to the doctors, he was not ill even now. He had seen three, unknown to Louise, apart from Dr. Maresco, their regular doctor, who lived two floors above them.

He had no confidence in this Rumanian, a mere boy, who smelled not of antiseptics but of the barbershop, and whose hands were white and carefully manicured. If old Dr. Rivet, who had been present at Louise's first communion and who had attended them since their marriage, had not died two years before, Etienne would have had nothing to worry about. "Make a note of the date of each attack and of what happened before," the doctor on Avenue des Ternes had said, though he sounded a bit skeptical.

This doctor, like the other two whom he had consulted without his wife's knowledge, he had chosen at random, selecting a district some distance away. Otherwise, one day when he was out with Louise, they might have met him. Then, supposing the doctor had greeted him, what explanation could he have given?

At any rate, when he gave up smoking, he had not yet begun to have those burning spasms in the throat, as he did now at the onset of an attack. Then, all he had felt was a certain dryness and some difficulty in swallowing, and at night, when he got into bed, waves of pain in his chest.

"Haven't you noticed anything?"

"No."

"I haven't had a cigarette all day."

"Oh!"

For three days he had kept a pack of cigarettes in his pocket. More than once, he had put one to his lips, but he had not lighted it.

"Well, there you are. That's that. I've finished with smoking."

That was on January 7 or 8. The seventh, because the evening before they had celebrated Twelfth-night with the Leducs. All evening, he had breathed in the fumes of Arthur Leduc's pipe, and it made him crave a cigarette more than ever. Still, his resolution brought a sense of relief. Now that he had given up smoking, these slight sensations of discomfort would disappear. He would get back his strength and begin to feel well again, better than ever, in fact.

At once, his appetite increased enormously, and for several weeks he ate almost twice as much as usual. He was the first to remark on it, jokingly:

"Have you noticed my appetite? It's incredible. If I go on like this, I'll be putting on weight."

He had never been fat, but he was not skinny, either. Now he was beginning to lose weight.

If he put his mind to it, retracing the course of events step by step, he might be able to recall all the dates. It was important to do so, he was sure. Then, still without saying anything to Louise, he would make an appointment with a specialist, one of the top men, who would go into his case thoroughly and settle the matter once and for all.

The one incident that he could not place in time was Françoise's telephone call. He could not remember whether it happened before or after Christmas, or even in February. All he knew was that it was sometime in the winter, and the days were short. They were having dinner together in the dining room, and their servant at the time was that girl from the south who always smelled of garlic. The telephone rang—at closing time, it was brought up to the apartment. It was almost always Louise who answered the telephone, and she did so on this occasion.

At first, he did not pay much attention to what she was saying. He assumed that it was Mariette Leduc on the line, particularly as he heard his wife say:

"Yes, I'm listening. What? Wait a minute. I can never remember the number. It's on Rue Saint-Georges. . . . Hold on."

She went to the drawer of the sewing machine, where she kept her personal papers, and opened it.

"Hello . . . Madame Bernard . . . Bernard. Yes, like the Christian name . . . number thirty-eight, Rue Saint-Georges."

It was the name of her dressmaker.

"No, she has no telephone. She's at home all day, except very early in the morning, when she does her shopping."

For the next few minutes, she listened, nodding, with an occasional monosyllable, then broke off:

"Good night, Françoise."

He was surprised. Françoise was his wife's sister. She was

married to a pharmacist, a man named Trivau, and lived on Rue de la Roquette. They had two daughters, one married to a teacher, the other, Armandine, still unmarried.

"Was that your sister on the phone?"

Nothing ever ruffled Louise. He had never seen her blush, or show the smallest sign of embarrassment. He could have sworn that the name of Françoise had slipped out inadvertently, and that, if it had not, she would have pretended that the caller was a customer. They had very few social contacts. In fact, except for the Leducs, they never saw anyone.

"She wanted the address of my dressmaker."

The Trivaus had completely broken with them more than fifteen years before. When they were first married, they had gone occasionally to Rue de la Roquette, two or three times possibly, and Etienne had always felt a little ill at ease there. The pharmacist's manner, in particular, was cold and distant.

Then one day, after Louise had been to see her sister on her own, she said when she got home:

"Good riddance!"

"What?"

"We won't have to see that pompous ass Trivau again."

"Did you quarrel?"

"I told him a few home truths."

That was all she had to say about it. They never saw them again. When, years later, the elder daughter, Charlotte, was married, they were not asked to the wedding, and only knew of it through the newspapers.

Louise had come back to the table and was finishing her meal. It was he who felt uncomfortable in pursuing the subject.

"Did you run into her somewhere?"

"Yes, a day or two ago."

Was it not rather strange that, having seen her sister again after so many years, she said nothing to him?

"What day?"

"I can't remember exactly. I'm sure I must have told you."

Except in the evening, when they went out to see a movie, or have a drink at an open-air café, or just stroll around the neighborhood, Louise virtually never left the house. It was she who managed the shop. She had done so since her father's death, as well as during the period of her first marriage. Etienne called on the customers. As for the dressmaker, Madame Bernard, she always came to the house for Louise's fittings.

"Did you meet her in the street?"

She did not seem to attach much importance to his questioning, and casually echoed his words.

"In the street, yes."

He dared not ask which street, but, guilefully assuming an innocent air, persisted:

"Was she going to see her daughter?"

"I expect so. She didn't say."

She was lying, and here was proof of it. They both knew, because they had been interested enough to consult the telephone book, that Charlotte lived behind the Luxembourg Gardens. To get to her daughter from Rue de la Roquette, Françoise had no need to come into the center of town. What could Louise have been doing without her husband's knowledge in the Bastille or Halle aux Vins district?

This question nagged at him. He had a horror of mysteries.

"Was she friendly?"

"Why shouldn't she have been?"

"Are you expecting to see her again?"

"I might. I don't know."

"What did she say about her husband?"

"We didn't talk about him."

What possible reason could Louise have, after almost sixteen years, to meet her sister again and, all at once, to be on such good terms with her as to exchange dressmakers' addresses?

Had his health begun to fail as far back as that? He searched his memory feverishly. At any rate, his first attack, his worst, had been in March.

They had finished dinner. It was a mild night, so they had left the window open, and he remembered seeing a flower seller on the boulevard at the corner of Place Blanche. They had had lentil soup, or, rather, he had, since his wife avoided starch. The significance of this struck him now for the first time. He almost got up to make a note of it in the Fabre book.

It had been past 9:30 when Louise went into the bedroom, and started to undress in a way that he had come to recognize as a kind of signal. From his armchair in the dining room, which they also used as their sitting room, he watched her, conscious all the while of the heaving of his stomach, troubled by the unfamiliar burning sensation that was mounting slowly from his chest to his throat.

He still believed then that it was an attack of indigestion, and it crossed his mind that it had come at an awkward moment.

Just then, two or three spasms of cramp clawed at his stomach. At the same time, sweat broke out on his forehead, and he was overcome with dizziness. His head swam. By now, Louise had finished undressing. His unseeing eyes were fixed on her naked body as she stood in the bedroom, in darkness except for the glow of light from the street.

He did not want to complain, but the burning in his throat was growing more and more distressing; then suddenly it seemed to him that his heart had stopped beating. In panic he gasped:

"Louise!"

She looked at him, surprised but unruffled.

"Aren't you feeling well?"

He was unable to speak now. It seemed to him that he would never be able to speak again. He made a movement with his right hand. She understood.

"Do you want a glass of water?"

He heard the bathroom tap running. He was impatient for her return. While she was out of his sight, his sense of danger seemed more acute.

The water brought him no relief. Louise was at his side, still naked. There was a kind of serenity in the full curves of her body, and repose in the whiteness of her skin.

When he raised his hand, once again she understood. She took his watch out of his pocket and felt his pulse.

"What is it?"

She hesitated, then said:

"It's not too bad."

With his eyes, he begged her to tell him the truth.

"Sixty-two."

He was certain that she was lying. Pressing his own fingers to his wrist, he was panic-stricken to feel the slowness of his heartbeats, and the long pauses in between.

"Call the doctor," he said in a low voice, as though it took all his strength to speak.

It had been the worst moment of his whole life. He had really thought that he was dying. His wife had called Olga, the maid at that time, who had not yet gone up to bed, and told her to run and fetch the doctor. As he lived in the building, it took less time than telephoning.

When Dr. Maresco had come down, Etienne was in the bathroom, vomiting. His wife, who had slipped on a blue dressing gown, was speaking in an undertone in the bedroom, saying:

"He had two plates of lentil soup for dinner. The attack came on suddenly, about twenty minutes ago."

"Is he subject to indigestion?"

"Not especially. He has it occasionally, like anyone else."

The doctor had examined him, had asked him his age and questioned him about his previous illnesses, and then scribbled a prescription.

"Send out for this medicine at once. I'll look in on him tomorrow morning."

Olga had run to the drugstore on Place Pigalle, which was open all night. Outside, the night life of the town was just beginning. Louise took his pulse again two or three times.

"Normal?"

"Almost."

"Didn't the doctor say anything to you when you showed him out?"

"Not a thing."

Next day, as he complained of feeling drained and listless, Maresco had prescribed a stimulant.

"I can't find anything organically wrong."

"What about my heart?"

"It was a bit sluggish last night. Probably due to indigestion. Are you the worrying kind?"

"Not in the least."

It was true.

"Are you a heavy smoker?"

"I gave it up two months ago."

He did not like Dr. Maresco, though he could not say why. Perhaps, like the concierge, he resented the kind of people he brought into the house. Though they might be living on Boulevard de Clichy, between Place Blanche and Place Pigalle, the tenants had never before had anything to do with the night life of the district.

It was only since Maresco had moved into an apartment on the fourth floor that women of a certain type were to be seen coming into the building, and invariably, in the elevator, pressing the fourth-floor button.

Louise had shown no sign of anxiety. He had kept to his room for just one day, and then resumed his round of calls on their Paris customers.

He covered most of the ground on foot, as the shopkeepers and small manufacturers with whom he did business were distributed in groups over three or four areas. His itinerary was planned in advance. He had known most of his customers for years, and had a regular day for calling on each of them.

On several occasions in the months that followed, he was seized in the street with the same sensation of dizziness, always accompanied by an unpleasant burning in the throat. He would come to a stop, and look sheepishly at the passers-by, who, it seemed to him, must all be aware that he was afraid he was going to die. Irrationally, he was reassured by the sight of a policeman in uniform.

Later, when he had calmed down, he would go into the nearest bar, and drink a glass of mineral water. There was another reason, too. Most bars had a mirror on the wall behind the bottles, and he wanted to take a look at himself. His appearance on these occasions was certainly most odd. His face was puffy, especially under the eyes, his pupils dilated, and his lips were compressed into a thinner line than usual.

Once, he had felt an attack coming on while they were playing cards with the Leducs, as they always did one evening a week. He had said, as casually as he could:

"Don't you think I'm looking a bit strange?"

Mariette Leduc had frowned with unmistakable concern. Her husband had shrugged his shoulders and said reassuringly:

"You could be a lot worse!"

As for Louise, she had looked at him steadily, and then said coolly:

"You're talking yourself into it."

All the same, she had taken his pulse and announced that it was normal.

The first two doctors he had gone to see had found it normal as well. He did not take them seriously. The one on Place de la République displayed a board as big as a shop sign, listing his scale of charges. His waiting room was crammed with shabby people. Etienne almost walked out before his turn came.

"Are you married?"

"Yes."

"Any children?"

"No."

"Is it you who can't?"

"It's my wife."

"How do you know?"

"Because she didn't have any by her first husband, either."

"What is your profession?"

He took his blood pressure.

"Do you often have these attacks?"

"Yesterday's was the ninth or tenth in four months."

"After meals?"

"One and a half to two hours after."

He prescribed a sedative.

As for the doctor on Rue Maubeuge, he had wanted him to come back for a more thorough examination, but he was so dirty and had such bad breath that Etienne could not bring himself to go to him again.

The most conscientious was the doctor on Avenue des Ternes. He was a little man, chubby and pink, with a bald head encircled by a sparse halo of reddish hair. He, too, had a steady stream of patients, mostly casual callers, but he happened to be a man as well as a doctor. Behind the thick lenses of his rimless spectacles, he had clear blue eyes, and during his examination, they were often fixed searchingly on Etienne's face.

When he had finished, he had asked:

"What are you afraid of?"

Etienne had not told him. Because he could not tell him, he stammered:

"Of being seriously ill."

"Is that all?"

It was touch and go. At that moment, the doctor was disposed to give him his full attention, to probe until he got to the root of the problem.

Etienne wondered why he had bothered to come, when, at the critical moment, all he could find to say, in the most offhand way, was:

"Well . . . of dying, of course."

That was not it. By then, there was more to it than that. He smiled as he said it, but, for all that, his lower lip trembled, and there was panic in his eyes.

"Have you noticed whether you are especially liable to these attacks in any particular circumstances?"

"What sort of circumstances?"

"Any special day of the week, for instance. Or after a long walk. Or after going up a lot of stairs. Or after a quarrel."

"I don't think so—my wife and I never quarrel."

Several times, as they talked, the little doctor seemed to be on the verge of giving him up, of going back to his waiting patients, as though to say:

"Well, if he won't talk!"

Each time—in spite of himself, it seemed—his glance came back to Etienne, and he was impelled to try again.

"If you are really worried, I would advise you, from now on, to make a note of *everything that happened before each attack, what you were doing, what you ate. . . .*"

He had had an attack that same afternoon, with only the iron staircase between himself and his wife, who was quite unaware of what was happening. He had not called her. He had not got up to fetch a glass of water. He had drunk a little lukewarm lemonade, which brought on a burning sensation in his stomach lasting several minutes.

Later, much later, he had written the few words now hidden inside the covers of *Social Life in the Insect World*.

The printing press down below had stopped. Monsieur Théo, with the deliberation and meticulous care with which he did everything, must now be changing from his long gray overall into his jacket.

In the absence of Monsieur Charles, it was Louise who, with an iron hook in her hand, pulled down the two metal shutters over the shop front.

He just had time to glance at the title of his Dumas novel. It was *Twenty Years After,* which he had read at least three times, so that he had time to skim through thirty pages or so.

2

He heard the click of the light switch downstairs, then his wife's footsteps on the stairs, and the knowledge that in a moment she would be there again, in the familiar surroundings that made their world, was enough to calm him in body and spirit, and make him feel ashamed of the evil thoughts that obsessed him when he was alone.

He knew what he would see: first, her mass of lustrous black hair, thick and flowing, not a strand out of place after a day at work; her face, full and serene, without a trace of fatigue, and her white-dotted black dress, as fresh as when she put it on, with its clinging bodice, and full skirt outlining the curve of her hips.

This was how she looked when she went down in the morning, and again after lunch, and how she still looked when she came upstairs in the evening, except for the two rings of sweat in her armpits, which he saw when she raised her arms, and whose faint tang he smelled when she bent over him.

She wore clothes of flowing, silky materials, which, with

every movement, revealed the maturity of her body, so that, as she went back and forth around him, he was always tempted to imagine her naked.

"How are you feeling?"

She did not smile, but not because she was anxious. She was simply being herself. They had lived together so long that their expressions no longer altered every time they met.

"All right. I'm sure my throat is less red."

She observed him, attentively and calmly, then went into the bathroom, switching on the light, to get the thermometer from the medicine chest. As she raised her arm, he saw the damp circle on her dress. It was an integral part of her, like the almost imperceptible dew which formed on her upper lip when they were out walking together in the summer sun, and which gave a distinctive flavor to their kisses.

Completely relaxed, she shook the thermometer, rinsed it under the tap, and came over to put it in his mouth. This was what she always did, morning and evening, each time he had the flu, and then, washing her hands and splashing water on her face, she watched him out of the corner of her eye, as though he were a child who might play tricks.

"It's starting to rain again. Just drizzle, the same as last night. There won't be many people at the fair."

The mercury in the thermometer had risen very little. In the morning Etienne's temperature had been barely 100°. This was not one of his worst bouts of the flu. It was more of a heavy cold in the head, with a stiff neck and cramp in the shoulder.

"What is it?"

"Under 100°."

She checked it mechanically, as, downstairs, she checked

the work of all the staff, even old Monsieur Théo, and then went toward the kitchen, where the maid could be heard clattering plates.

He knew where and when he had caught cold. The previous Sunday afternoon had been sunny, with hot gusts of wind, and they had walked as far as the Tuileries. There was an exhibition of Dutch paintings in the Jeu de Paume Pavilion, and they had visited it. They enjoyed going to exhibitions, moving slowly through the crowd, stopping in front of each painting. It was hot in the picture gallery, and Etienne had perspired.

When they came out, at about five o'clock, the sun was setting, but the air was still warm. They had walked toward Rue Royale, stopping for an apéritif at an open-air café. They had said very little. They never talked a great deal, yet they were very conscious of being two people, a little set apart from the rest, as they watched the crowds moving slowly along the sidewalk.

"Where shall we have dinner?"

This question came up every Sunday evening. As it was the girl's night out, they always dined at a restaurant, and they liked to make the most of it.

"We haven't been to Place des Victoires for ages."

They knew a quiet and comfortable corner restaurant that smelled of good cooking and Calvados.

"Fine."

They walked on, along the great boulevards, which were now brilliantly lit, with people lining up outside the movie houses. Place des Victoires, deserted and lit only by the street lamps and the glow from their little restaurant, seemed to them, in contrast, provincial.

There were six tables set out on the terrace under the

orange awning, flanked by two rows of green plants, and the electric light, filtering through a milky globe, recalled the lighting of an earlier day.

Only one couple was dining out of doors, a boy and a girl in love, for whom it was an exhilarating experience to be there together, and who, for no reason but that they were happy, looked at the older couple with eyes full of merriment, while the boy's hand closed more firmly on his companion's thigh, a large, very noticeable hand, paler than the girl's dress.

Louise had said:

"Shall we eat outside?"

That was what she wanted, and he knew why. If she understood him, he, too, in the course of time, had come to know many of her little secrets.

Normally, knowing Etienne's susceptibility to colds, she would have insisted that they sit indoors.

It was not the shadowy square, still and empty as in an engraving, that attracted her. Perhaps she did not realize what was happening within herself. He had divined it a long time ago, though he had never spoken of it to her; indeed, he had never even tried to put it into words.

There was a connection with the curtains she left open at night, as though she needed the life outside to share in her passion.

Often, too, especially on hot summer days, she did not go downstairs immediately after lunch. The two bedroom windows were wide open, screened from the house opposite by the leaves of tall trees. But, lying in bed, they only had to raise their heads a little to see the crowds and the cars. The cream-colored top of the bus going by was almost on a level with them, and the noises of the town with, here and there, an individual voice isolated and distinct, enveloped them, like the muffled sounds of nature in the country.

She said, without much conviction:

"Won't you be cold?"

"Of course not."

But for the pair of lovers, she would have preferred to sit indoors. She chose the wicker chair facing them, and all through dinner he knew that she was watching them, as though she were plumbing their depths. He recognized the revealing break in her voice, and was moved by it, because it betrayed the warmth and impatience of her body.

Just once, she noticed that he was shivering.

"You're in a draft. We'd better change places."

He had agreed to this only right at the end, over dessert, realizing that she wanted him to see them as well, so that she could watch his eyes following the young man's large hand caressing the girl's flesh.

The truth was that he and Louise were in some way accomplices, and the young man must have sensed this, because he grew more and more audacious, and at the same time looked straight at them with a challenging expression. Had he noticed, too, that Louise's lips had grown intensely red, and were pursed in a more sensual curve?

They went home by bus. The journey was an interlude during which they were both absorbed in preserving the full intensity of the inward excitement that had swept over them on the terrace.

There had been many such moments in their life, a shared, subtle pleasure in going through the archway, up the badly lit stairs, fitting the key into the lock, being met by the familiar smell of home, and at last coming to their own secret domain.

Louise went into the bedroom first, while he bolted the door. She waited for the familiar sound before taking off her hat, as though she felt impelled to keep an eye on Etienne.

She had not turned on the light. He had been certain beforehand that she would not. The lights of the fair, which was going full blast, were circling around the room, vibrant with the sounds of jumbled music, whistle blasts, the fortuneteller's buzzer, and the shrieks of the girls in the bumper cars.

Louise was undressing slowly. It was like a sunrise: her rounded shoulders, her arms, then her thighs glimmering in the half-light, at last her whole body seeming to fill the room with life, intense and warm.

Her voice was different, too, a voice unlike that of any other woman he had ever known, when she called out:

"Come!"

He knew that the lovers on the terrace had a part in their embraces, and other couples, too, whom they had caught sight of briefly during the day, and their passion was spiced with eddies of desire snatched from the air of the town, and with all the animal excitement of the fairground.

When they lay back, side by side, they were drained of everything, feeling nothing but a blissful emptiness, and each kept a hand on the other's body, no matter where, just so as not to break the contact.

Only later, just before going to sleep, had Etienne asked himself, as he had done often before during the past months, whether his wife was as she had always been, whether there was not some change in her demeanor.

It was important. The notion that she might not be quite the same had come to him after his first attack, and he had thought to begin with that it was he who, shrinking from further discomfort, had not behaved exactly as usual.

After that, he had begun to watch her every movement and, with his cheek against hers, and his eyes closed, to listen to the changing rhythm of her breathing, alert to the slightest tremor of her flesh.

Afterward, he would brood over it, especially when he was alone. In her presence, he felt ashamed, as tonight he felt ashamed of the slip of paper hidden in *Social Life in the Insect World*.

It was not only shame, but fear as well, fear so compelling that he almost took advantage of his wife's absence in the kitchen to get up and destroy the sheet of writing paper. Would she not notice that the book with the green cover had been moved? Or might she not, that very evening, just happen to take it out unthinkingly, to look at the illustrations? She had never done so. But suppose the word "insect" were to crop up in conversation, then might it not occur to her to consult Fabre as one would an encyclopedia?

His mood had changed little by the morning after the Sunday at the Tuileries. He had awakened with a hot forehead and a slight stiffness in the neck, and he had not said anything.

It was raining. His wife had said, "You ought to take your raincoat."

He would have felt too hot. It was a close day. His case was heavy: though most of the time he called only on regular customers, it was common practice to carry samples.

She had made out a list for him. It was at the cashier's desk, in the morning, that they said good-by to each other, and at these times she treated him like an employee.

The stationer's shop belonged to her. Her father's name was still over the door, her maiden name was printed on the letter headings and bills. She briefed him no less minutely than she would, say, Jean-Louis, the delivery boy, who made the rounds on the carrier-tricycle, though she would not have dared to use the same tone with Monsieur Théo, who had worked in the printing office in her father's day.

Downstairs, he was nobody, and he knew it. The district he was to cover that day, the Barbès district, was the one he liked least. It was not worth taking the bus or subway. It was no distance away. The streets seemed to him more dingy than most, and almost his entire route was uphill.

All morning, his forehead felt hot, and he was anticipating an attack. Passing the home of one of the three doctors made him feel more low-spirited than ever. By eleven o'clock, his legs seemed to be giving way under him, and while he was with one of his customers, a dairyman who could barely read or write, he felt a sharp pain in his neck as he turned his head.

He did not return home at once, but finished his morning round, dragging his feet, then had a cup of coffee in a bistro and, glancing at himself in the mirror, saw that he was looking ill.

It was not until he was going up the iron staircase that he decided he must have the flu. Louise was upstairs already. In the lunch hour, Monsieur Charles stayed in the shop and, sitting at the counter in the back, ate sandwiches that he brought with him in a lunch box.

"Anything wrong?"

Coming suddenly into the warm room, he had sneezed and blown his nose. He was very flushed.

"There now, you've caught a cold."

She had gone to get the thermometer. His temperature was slightly above normal.

"You're going to bed."

Why had he had the feeling that it suited her to put him

to bed? It was not the first time that he had the flu, and her treatment never varied.

"Let me look at your throat."

He did have a sore throat.

"Have you got any lemons, Fernande? No? Well, straight after lunch, go and get a dozen."

Fernande was not used to things yet. She was new in the house. None of the maids stayed long. He had never asked himself why. His wife always picked the same type, plump country girls coming to work in Paris for the first time. She must get them through an agency, he supposed.

"So you finished your round all the same? Wouldn't you have done better to come home right away?"

Because of his evil thoughts, he dared not look at her. She would see through him. These thoughts had harassed him a good deal lately. He had tried to fight them off, even going so far as to tell himself they were just part of his indisposition.

Besides, it was all very vague. It was not, as one might have supposed, altogether a matter of jealousy. All the same, he could not help wondering whether there had ever been times when Louise had felt she wanted another man, whether she ever felt it now.

For more than fifteen years he had lived with her, and this thought had never crossed his mind. Why should it suddenly strike him now? When had it first occurred to him? He had no idea. It must have been about the time his attacks began, in February or March. And always, when he allowed himself to dwell on it, the name of Françoise came to mind.

Why had his wife lied to him about her sister? How, in what circumstances, and, above all, for what purpose had the two women come together again after so many years?

The episode on the terrace the previous evening was not unique. The same kind of thing had happened more than once in the past. Why, then, did he find it so disturbing? It was, after all, in his arms that she had satisfied her desire.

If she had found herself alone with the young man on the terrace, would it have ended differently?

As they were finishing lunch on that Monday afternoon, she had said, before putting him to bed:

"It will do you good to have a rest."

"Do you think I'm looking tired?"

He was growing distressingly sensitive. He suspected a hidden meaning in the most straightforward remark. Perhaps because he was beginning to feel his age? Was that the reason? He was past forty, and his last birthday had affected him more than any of the others, as though it had been a decisive turning point.

But Louise herself was forty-six. It was incredible. He could have sworn that she had not changed, that she was as he had always known her. All the same, she was six years older than he.

Had she not reached the age when a woman most longed to recapture youth?

"What are you thinking about?"

"Nothing. I don't know."

She repeated the same question now, turning her steady, tranquil gaze on him. They were never so cozily together as when he had the flu and they were confined within the four walls of the bedroom.

His dinner had been brought to him in bed on a tray, while Louise had hers at an occasional table where the radio set usually stood. She had undressed, and was wearing her dressing gown of heavy blue silk, with its deep, revealing neckline.

"Are you reading *Twenty Years After?*"

"I've started it."

"But you read it last year!"

She must have guessed that he had something on his mind, but did not know what it was. If she made up her mind to find out, she would.

Caution was essential. He must try to be rational. All day he had been alert to every sound in the shop, telling himself that there might be some man who came to see Louise when he was out. Had she had any opportunity to let him know that Etienne was ill and staying indoors?

"Didn't Monsieur Charles come in today?" he asked, as though he did not care one way or the other.

For now everything was open to suspicion. Monsieur Charles, the stockman, whose surname was Laboine, had come to the shop before he himself had, even before Louise's first husband. He must be fifty now, but he was an ageless man. He must always have been as gentle, as humble as he was now, with his graying fair hair, his light-blue eyes, his face, which was a little dried up but not wrinkled. He reminded one of a sheep. For a long time, he had lived on Rue Caulaincourt, a few yards from the shop; then, after the birth of his third or fourth child, he had bought a detached house in the suburbs, near Issy-les-Moulineaux.

In the shop, instead of a gray overall like Monsieur Théo, he wore a biscuit-colored one that almost matched his hair.

"I gave him the afternoon off for his granddaughter's christening."

"I didn't know any of his children were married."

"Two sons and a daughter."

So she had been by herself downstairs. From his glass cage, Monsieur Théo could see most of the shop, but the left-hand corner was out of his range of vision.

If she were seeing another man, could Etienne have sensed it? What changes would it have made in her? Would she have been able to look at him in the same way, to speak to him in the same tone of voice?

He had believed that he knew her, but here he was now, incapable of guessing her thoughts.

His body felt hot and sticky under the sheets. Fernande was clearing the dishes, and as she bent over him, he was aware of the smell of a woman's body different from that to which he was accustomed. There was no bathroom on the sixth floor where the maid slept, and she probably did not wash too often. Her breast touched his shoulder, her uncombed hair brushed against him, and he only thought the more about Louise.

The more uneasy he felt, the more he was prone to sudden gusts of desire. There was an element of spite in it, too. It was difficult to explain. It was as though to possess her body were not simply an assertion of his rights, but also a kind of revenge.

He knew that she was going to take a book from the top shelf, a book with a yellow or white cover, and that she would settle down opposite him in the armchair. If it had not been for the racket of the fair, she would have switched on the radio.

"Are you all right?"

"Yes," he said, with his hand on the Dumas.

"You can go up after you've finished the dishes, Fernande. Don't forget to turn off the gas."

The girl gave a nod and a grunt in reply, and went without

saying good night. It was typical of her. When her work was done, she went up to her room, and, in the morning, came down with swollen, bleary eyes and a powerful smell of bed.

Half an hour later, they would hear the landing door shut. Louise would get up to go and bolt it, passing through the kitchen to make sure that everything was in order.

He opened his book. His wife opened hers. Instead of reading, though he was careful to turn a page now and again, he went on brooding over her state of mind.

The question that obsessed him was: how would she behave in the arms of another man? Would an affair leave any mark on her? It was absurd, yet he was actually thinking of some kind of physical mark, because he could not bring himself to believe that it could leave her quite unscathed.

At once, he began to compile a sort of private inventory of her body.

He recalled the two occasions when he himself had been unfaithful, only two in fifteen years—or, rather, the two occasions when he had tried to be unfaithful.

The first time was with the servant they had then, a girl not unlike Fernande, seventeen or eighteen years old, very plump, who, right through the summer, wore the same pink dress. He knew that she was naked under it, because from time to time the skirt would get caught up between her buttocks.

They had been married for three years. It happened one morning. Louise had gone to the funeral of a friend of her father's, leaving Etienne in charge of the shop.

Monsieur Charles had been there, wearing his brownish overall, and Monsieur Théo, too, in his glass-walled printing office. On her return from the market, the girl, whose name was Charlotte, had come in through the shop instead of under the archway—he could no longer remember why, probably because she had some message for him—and he had watched her going up the iron staircase.

For ten minutes or so he had stayed there thinking about her, and his body had grown clammy then, as it was now under the sheets. Louise would not be back for at least an hour, as the funeral was taking place at the Montparnasse Cemetery.

"I'll be back right away, Monsieur Charles."

Foolishly, since there was a huge clock in a black case directly opposite him, he had added:

"I left my watch upstairs."

He had gone up without making a sound. No sooner had he reached the top of the stairs than he almost started down again. His sense of guilt was so intense that it made his heart pound and his hands tremble.

The kitchen door was open. Charlotte, in her pink dress, was standing at the table covered in oilcloth, scraping asparagus.

She had watched him coming toward her as though she had been expecting what was to follow. He had moved behind her, still hesitating, then suddenly he had gripped her by the buttocks with both hands.

She had not even let go of the knife she was holding. She had merely leaned forward, and then—through fear, perhaps —he had been seized with giddiness. Feverishly, and with knees trembling, he was yet stubbornly determined to go through with it, but at last, defeated, he had gone out of the room without a word.

Charlotte had remained in their service for two months after that, and for two months he had lived in terror, no longer daring even to look at her.

She had not given him away, even when Louise had fired her, following the disappearance of some trifling sum of money.

This particular experience had been quite enough to last him for years, and though he might sometimes savor the attractions of another woman at a distance, it was to his wife that he always turned for fulfillment.

The second time had been almost a romance. One winter afternoon, at about five o'clock, with melting snow falling and the roads tacky with slush, he had gone into a bar near the Châteaudun crossroads, to have a cup of hot coffee.

There was a young woman opposite him, leaning her elbows on the counter. Once or twice their glances had met, and he could tell that she was not a prostitute. A typist, perhaps, or, more probably, a small-time dancer?

She was attractively dressed. Her fair hair was fluffed out under her red hat.

He was not sure which of them had been the first to smile. Strangely moved, he had wanted to speak to her, to hear the sound of her voice.

"Cigarette?" he had said at last, holding out his case to her. At that time, he was still a smoker.

She had taken one. He remembered her polished fingernails. He had felt uncomfortable. Even before his marriage he had seldom found himself in a situation of this kind and, having no idea of what he was expected to say, was very conscious of his own awkwardness, which she seemed to find amusing.

"Are you a typist?"

"I'm an actress."

Small parts, no doubt. A chorus girl, perhaps.

"Near here?"

"Just now, I'm rehearsing at the Théâtre Saint-Georges."

"What would you like to drink?"

She had had an apéritif. He drank one with her, and later explained it to Louise by saying that he had met some non-existent crony.

He had really wanted that young woman, not as he had wanted the maid, but to hold in his arms and stroke tenderly.

"Are you free?"

"What do you mean?"

"Do you have a few minutes to spare?"

"What for?"

He had merely smiled, and only then had she said:

"Where?"

He had no idea. He was not familiar with any of the hotels in the district, and was afraid that, if they went into one at random, they might be refused a room. Out in the street with her, he was already beginning to feel frightened.

"Are you married?"

"Yes."

"Is your wife jealous?"

"I should imagine so."

He remembered a corridor with cream-colored walls and a red-carpeted staircase, a chambermaid who unlocked a door for them, with the announcement:

"I'll bring you your towels."

His companion had stood in the middle of the room, waiting, then, with a slight shrug, had started to undress.

She had a pleasing though not very taut body, with a cluster of little spots on one shoulder.

Twenty minutes or so went by. Then she said softly:

"What's wrong with you?"

"I don't know."

She had tried to help him, gently and kindly. It was he who had put an end to it.

"Please forgive me."

"It's not your fault."

He had never tried again. He could see her still very clearly, and she was really pretty and touching, with freckles down the sides of her nose.

With her, he had been impotent, yet the mere sight of his wife's blue dressing gown, clinging to her rounded body, was enough to make him tense with impatience.

He knew what was going to happen. So did she. Maybe she was not really concentrating on her book. She knew him so well.

"Is it interesting?" he asked, in a voice that did not sound quite like his own.

"What?"

"What you're reading."

"It's well written."

Had it ever happened to her? Had she ever tried with other men? Had it worked for her?

"Louise."

"Yes."

She pretended not to understand, but he could have sworn that her thighs were moist already. He was always more ardent when he was feverish. His senses were intensely sharpened. Things were not the same between them as at other times.

He hated himself for having called her, it was too much like a cry for help. He hated himself for the spitefulness underlying his desire, and for his surrender, his cowardice.

Again, he said:

"Louise!"

This time, she half looked up to say:

"Yes?"

It was his turn now to whisper, without looking at her:

"Will you?"

It was a relief when she turned out the light, because his eyes were smarting with tears.

3

Next morning, when his wife removed the thermometer from his mouth, and took it to the window to read, he asked:

"What is it?"

Before she replied, he could have sworn that he was less well than he had been the night before, and he had a violent headache.

"98°."

"Are you sure?"

"See for yourself."

He believed her. It was humiliating to find that his temperature was actually below normal, and that he did not have the flu. To make up for it, however, his cold was worse, his nose red, and his eyes feverishly bright.

"You'd better stay in bed and get rid of that cold. Anyway, you can't possibly go out. It will be soon enough if you get up this evening in time for the Leducs."

It was Thursday, the day when, each week, Mariette and Arthur Leduc came in for dinner and a game of cards.

It was overcast out of doors, but not raining. The muslin curtains were so transparent that people and things moving in the street were clearly visible, though as if through a light mist. The roofs of the fairground booths were still wet and shining, the tents were dripping, smoke was rising from caravan chimneys, and there were children sitting on steps eating, most of them with mops of disheveled hair, and dressed in ill-fitting clothes.

Etienne had perspired so much in the night that, at about three, Louise had made him change his pajamas, and the bed was still impregnated with the smell of his sweat, which he inhaled surreptitiously, while keeping an eye on his wife, who was moving around the room getting dressed. This was something he had never confessed to her or to anyone; it was a secret known only to one person in all the world—his liking for the smell of his own perspiration.

One summer morning, when he was a little boy of five or six, it had come to him as a revelation when he had sniffed at the back of his hand, and inhaled the smell rising from his hot, moist skin. It gave him pleasure, and he was blowing on his hand, to warm it, when his mother caught him at it.

"What are you doing?"

Her reproving manner had so shaken him that he had lied instinctively.

"Nothing. I hurt my hand and I was just licking it."

"That's a dirty thing to do," she had said.

A little later, after he had started learning the catechism, he had come to believe that the word "dirty," as used by his mother, did not refer to physical cleanliness, but that what he had done that day belonged to the mysterious realm of the sins of the flesh.

"Are you going to have a bath?" asked Louise.

Because, if so, she would not let the water drain. He did not find it distasteful to wash in her bath water. The water heater was sluggish, and emitted an unpleasant whistling sound.

"I think I will."

"I'll tell Fernande to change the sheets." Louise went downstairs just in time to open the back door to Monsieur Théo, whom they could see from the window as he came out of the subway station; and the stockman, who arrived immediately after him, raised the shutters over the shop front. The house and the town came to life simultaneously, as Fernande went over the apartment with the vacuum cleaner, and the housewives of the neighborhood crowded around the fruit and vegetable barrows all along Rue Lepic.

Standing naked in the bathroom, Etienne looked at himself in the mirror, and saw that he had lost still more weight. His ribs were beginning to show, and it seemed to him that his skin was a bleached, unhealthy color. He cut himself shaving and had to stop several times to wipe away the blood.

When he went back to bed, the housework was still in progress, and for a time the maid was in the room, moving around near the bed. It occurred to him, then, to wonder what she thought of him, of both of them, and of their life together, enacted within the narrow confines of the apartment, with the same view from all the windows, and, except for the Leducs, no contact with the rest of the world. To stop himself from brooding, he opened his Dumas, and tried to concentrate on it once more.

After reading a few pages, he was saddened by a thought that had not occurred to him when he had read the book before. Resuscitating in *Twenty Years After* the characters who in *The Three Musketeers* were about twenty years old, Dumas portrayed them almost as old men, or at any rate as men whose active lives were over. And these people were about his own age.

Every time the telephone rang downstairs, he strained his ears.

"Yes, of course, Monsieur Peyre. Your order is ready. I'll definitely have it delivered this morning."

She did not always address her callers by name. When she did not, he tried to identify them from what she was saying.

Was it not strange that Françoise, at her age, had no dressmaker of her own, and had to call her sister to get the address of hers? There was no doubt that she had telephoned from home. At that time of the evening, her husband was in. He, too, must have been puzzled by the call, after such a long estrangement.

Etienne was itching to make fresh notes on the sheet of paper hidden in the Fabre book. He felt that it would help him, if only to get rid of a suspicion that crossed his mind from time to time and that frightened him. During his boyhood in Lyons, there had been a man living on the same street who had made such a deep impression on him that he could still remember him more clearly than his own father. He was a very tall, cadaverous man, who had seemed old to him then, but who, in fact, must have been about his own age today. He had a little pointed beard, and always carried a black walking stick. Presumably he did no work, as he could be seen around the street at all hours of the day, walking like an automaton, staring straight ahead, speaking to no one, greeting no one, stopping dead when he came to a group of children playing on the sidewalk, and then deliberately walking around them.

He had heard his parents saying to each other:

"He's a neurotic."

His mother had added:

"That poor wife of his. She leads the life of a martyr."

He did not want to be a neurotic. The thought terrified him. He remembered his mother's shocked tone as she spoke the word. He was not imagining things. Why, if there was nothing wrong, had the doctor on Avenue des Ternes advised him to take notes? Why had he been losing weight visibly during the past few months? Why was he always tired and apathetic? Why was he breathless going up stairs? He was only forty, and there was nothing organically wrong with him, or so they said.

The impulse was becoming irresistible. He waited until there were several customers in the shop, then, seizing his chance, got out of bed without a sound, took the sheet of paper from *Social Life in the Insect World,* and, realizing that he had nothing significant to add, contented himself with filling in the exact date, writing "September 23" next to "Tuesday." He was unlikely to have an attack today. So far he had never had two so close together.

His wife had not heard him get up. As he went back to bed, he heard her talking to Jean-Louis, the delivery boy.

"I've told you before, it's in the left-hand corner of the warehouse," she said, not without impatience.

"No, madame, it's not."

"I saw it myself only the day before yesterday."

"Well, I've had a good look there."

"Come along with me, I'll show you. That will teach you not to be so cocksure."

The idea struck him as absurd. All the same, he followed them in his imagination, first going to the back of the shop, where it was very dark, then through the door leading to the courtyard, and crossing it with them.

The warehouse, where all the bulkier stock was kept, was an old stable block with coach-house doors. As these were heavy, a small door had been cut in the one on the left. Inside, there was a pervasive smell of cardboard and glue. The only light came from a naked bulb, thick with dust, dangling from a length of cord.

He had not thought of this. Today, Monsieur Charles was not celebrating his granddaughter's christening. He was down there. Etienne had heard him. Why then had his wife taken the trouble to go to the warehouse herself, instead of sending him with Jean-Louis?

He tried to remember how long the boy had been working for them. Whereas they seldom kept a maid for more than two or three months, the delivery boys usually stayed for about a year. When they first came, they were just kids, and Louise treated them as such; but as time went on they began to grow up, sprouting bristles on the chin, turning into men, looking for another job. Jean-Louis must have been with them for six months or so. He was the son of the concierge next door. Louise had known his mother before he was born, and later had seen him, as a baby, left for hours on the stoop, and Etienne could remember him playing with his friends among the trees of the boulevard.

It was really too far-fetched, he decided, but, all the same, he reverted to it several times in the course of the day.

At noon, when his wife came upstairs for lunch, two of his handkerchiefs were sodden and his eyelids were itching.

"You're not bored, are you?"

"No."

"It's too hot in here. I think I'd better open the window."

"If you think it's all right . . ."

He was none too pleased, because the breeze blowing in and the street noises, suddenly much clearer, made it harder for him to concentrate on his own thoughts.

He had wondered, that morning, what Fernande thought of him. During lunch, he kept looking at his wife, wondering what other men thought of her. She saw a great many, customers and salesmen. In fact, she saw more people than he did, although she seldom left the house.

He could not have said whether she was beautiful. He had never considered the question. Up to now, it had not mattered. She was his wife. They were bound together as closely as two people could possibly be. Was it not astounding that, in a capital city the size of Paris, there were only two people, the Leducs, who, once a week, shared in their private life?

Apart from the Leducs and the maid, besides the plumber, the decorator, and the glazier, he could not think of anyone who had ever been asked into their apartment.

In the evenings, when the weather was fine, there were just the two of them, strolling around the neighborhood for a breath of air, keeping pace with the people out exercising their dogs. On Sunday, too, there were still just the two of them, going to the movies, occasionally in summer to the country, and even then they were still in some sense insulated, always impatient to return home, to shut themselves in and get back to their secret life together.

What did it matter whether Louise was beautiful or not, since she was his partner in all this?

What use could there be in knowing how she looked to other men?

For him, her every movement, every fold in her dress, was evocative.

What of the salesmen, for instance, who called at intervals to get orders, and whom, after a time, she got to know quite well—did any of them ever pay her a compliment? When she leaned over the counter, her breasts showing, did they respond with a rush of desire?

If so, she must have been conscious of it.

Could there be some among them who had paid court to her? He was never there. Perhaps one or another, bolder than the rest, had made her a proposition?

She had never mentioned any such thing, never alluded to the way men behaved toward her.

Was there much comfort in reminding himself that she was forty-six? The truth was that he would have been happier if she had been ugly, or at least if she had appeared ugly, or better still, unattractive to others.

At about three o'clock, a smell of food pervaded the apartment, and he could tell that it was rabbit cooking. As she did every Thursday, Louise came upstairs several times to supervise the dinner. She did not trust Fernande to manage on her own.

Was he imagining things, or was his wife more abstracted than usual?

"You'll just put on your dressing gown, I suppose?"

"I'd rather get dressed."

"As you like."

He had a strong sense of propriety. He simply could not have sat down to dinner with the Leducs in his dressing gown. He got dressed too early. He no longer felt like reading. He roamed around the apartment, unable to settle anywhere. They could have had a sitting room; there was a spare room. It had been Louise's in her parents' time. The furniture was still there, stacked against the back wall. For years, the room had been used as a repository for unsalable stock that could not be kept downstairs.

They had no need of a sitting room. They had installed two armchairs in the dining room, and they sat in there when they were not in their bedroom.

The fairground music had started up again, but things were not very lively. There were only two or three bumper cars in use, and the young man in the white sweater, going round and round on the swings, was a solitary figure.

There was a strip of light showing under the kitchen door. Etienne felt so lonely that he almost went in, just to be with another human being.

From time to time he went to the head of the iron staircase, and listened. For no reason, he was in a state of mounting agitation. So much so that he wondered whether he was going to have an attack. He was reminded of a man, another neighbor in Lyons, who had died, all alone, without a sound, sitting at the table set for dinner, while his wife was in the kitchen, putting the finishing touches on the meal. When she came back, carrying the soup tureen, she stumbled over his bulky body, stretched out on the floor.

There was five minutes' difference between the alarm clock in the bedroom and the clock in the shop. Downstairs, it was ten to six. Between attending to customers, they were tidying the counters.

It seemed to him that it would never end. Standing there, he followed every detail of the closing-time routine, and when at last Louise came toward the stairs, he tiptoed to an armchair, so that she would not find him watching for her return.

She never changed her dress for the Leducs. Just as she

did every evening when they were alone, she washed her hands and face, and applied fresh powder, and a few drops of eau de cologne behind the ears.

"What was Jean-Louis looking for in the warehouse?"

He had sworn to himself that he would not mention it. He had been mistaken. She did not start or turn around to look at him. All the same, he sensed that she was surprised.

"You heard?"

She knew that what was said at the desk could be heard in the bedroom.

"The ledgers for Portman's," she went on. "He said they weren't there."

"I know."

"They were, of course, all packed and labeled. Only Monsieur Charles had stacked some boxes on top of them, and Jean-Louis hadn't thought of moving them."

Fernande was setting the table and getting the tray of drinks ready. Louise was going to and fro between the dining room and the kitchen. She took the bottle of vermouth from the sideboard, and uncorked the Bordeaux.

"Have you heard anything more from your sister?"

"No. Why should I?"

"I don't know. Since you've made up with her, she might have telephoned."

"Because we just happened to run into each other, it doesn't mean that we're back on the old footing."

He ought not to have persisted. There were some days like that, when he did everything he should not have done, and, because he was aware of it, he was all the more furious with himself.

"You haven't taken your temperature again?"

"No."

"Well, take it now."

He took the thermometer out of his mouth, as the Leducs rang at the door. He had no fever: 98°. Still below normal.

Fernande went to open the door, then Louise went to meet them, and he could hear Mariette's laugh.

"What did I tell you, Arthur?"

She explained in her high-pitched voice:

"I had a bet with Arthur that we'd be having rabbit."

"Why?"

"It's in season. You always give us rabbit at least once in September."

"Don't you like it?"

"I love it."

The two women kissed. Mariette usually kissed Etienne as well, on both cheeks. She had to stand on tiptoe, as she was very short.

"Have you got a cold?"

She made a joke of everything. She never kept still for a moment, and because she was plump, a good deal fatter than Louise, with light, rather puffy skin, his wife had once remarked:

"She doesn't walk. She rolls."

As for Arthur, he came in without fuss, not saying a word, his thin lips stretched in his usual fixed smile, and winked at Etienne by way of greeting.

"Feeling all right?"

To all intents and purposes, he had never left Montmartre. Mariette was born above the fish shop on Rue Lepic. They still got their fish there, though it was no longer run by her parents.

Louise and she had played together as children, had gone to the same school, and later to the same convent.

In fact, the Thursday dinner party was an established custom before Etienne's marriage, so that Arthur Leduc had, in a sense, been there longer than Etienne.

"Vermouth?"

"Cassis," Mariette's husband said.

And, in that instant, Etienne intercepted an exchange of looks between the two women. It was Mariette who had looked questioningly at Louise, and he could have sworn that his wife had shaken her head almost imperceptibly in reply, as though to say:

"Don't worry."

Suddenly, he was blushing furiously, and to cover it up, he took out his handkerchief. He must put it out of his mind for the time being, or he would give himself away.

"Has the child a cold?" asked Arthur, in his usual facetious manner.

It was an affectation with him, like his way of holding a cigarette and blowing out the smoke. He was no longer young. He must have been forty-eight or forty-nine, but he did not, and probably never would, behave like a grown man.

"Here's to your good health, my dears," said Louise.

Arthur made his usual reply:

"Here's to mine!"

Once again, while they all had their glasses raised, Etienne thought he saw the two women exchange glances. As Fernande was going past, Louise asked:

"Can we start dinner, Fernande?"

"It won't be more than ten minutes, madame."

There was a pause. Later, if he had been able to draw, Etienne could have reconstructed the scene in every detail. He could still see the four people, or, rather, five, counting the back view of the maid on her way to the kitchen.

The lighting in the dining room, which was rustic in style, was provided by an old cartwheel fitted with electric bulbs. It was a dim, yellowish light. The tablecloth this evening was yellow, too. No one was sitting down. Arthur, in a brown suit, his glass in his hand, was leaning against the dresser, against a background of gaudy earthenware plates.

Louise was wearing a black dress, Etienne's favorite, because it was molded to her hips. She was putting her glass down on the sideboard, after having drunk from it. Mariette, small, chubby, and fair-haired, wearing a green dress, was watching her.

There had been a moment of silence; then Louise had said, in what seemed to her husband a strained voice:

"Come into the bedroom, I've got something to show you."

Etienne did not move. He, too, was holding a glass, and he had his handkerchief in the other hand. There was a buzzing in his head. He looked at them, stunned, then followed them to the door. He was still hoping that he might be mistaken when, as though it were the most natural thing in the world, Louise shut the door.

A voice behind him, heavily sarcastic as ever, said:

"The boss wants to talk secrets with Mariette."

Etienne could not reply. He was as incapable of uttering a word as he was of taking his eyes off the door, behind which they could hear whispering. The clink of dishes was coming from the kitchen. The fairground music drifted in intermittently. It all seemed unreal. It belonged to the present, to events not yet fully enacted.

What seemed more real to him was a voice, his own, which he thought he could hear, and Mariette's, at the other end of the line.

"You will tell her?"

"I promise."

He had the feeling that she was smiling, making fun of him, perhaps. At any rate, she was undoubtedly amused at his feverish tone.

"When?"

"I'll speak to her later."

"Why not right away?"

"Because I was just going to get dressed. I'm stark naked."

It conjured up no image. It was just Mariette, and her body meant nothing to him.

"In five minutes?"

"Let's say ten."

"Can I call you back in a quarter of an hour?"

He was in the bar on the corner of Rue Lepic and Boulevard de Clichy, and, as he left the telephone booth, he could see the dark frontage of the stationer's shop. It was spring, a brilliantly sunny day. There were flies buzzing around the bar.

Snorting with impatience, he barked at the proprietor, who was standing there in his shirt sleeves, looking at him inquiringly.

"Give me another."

He was wearing a new suit, which he had bought the day before on one of the main boulevards, puffing nervously at his cigarette, staring at the clock, which had little flowers around the dial. The bistro smelled of spirits. Outside, there was a small barrow, piled high with cherries. The housewives were chattering loudly.

He was twenty-four years old. The minutes dragged on endlessly, and he kept fidgeting with the winder of his wristwatch.

His second apéritif made him a little lightheaded, just enough to add a kind of vibrancy to the atmosphere, to heighten the pitch of living, so that everything, the passers-by, the proprietor's blue apron, the street noises, the clinking glasses, the smells, his own person reflected in the mirror, tense, desperate to succeed, were all blended in a dazzling symphony, with the sun clashing the cymbals.

He saw his hand pushing the glass across the wet metal counter.

"Another?" a voice said.

It did not matter whose voice it was or where it came from. It did not matter whether or not it was the voice of the proprietor with the Burgundian accent. It was magnificent.

"Another! And a telephone token."

It seemed to him that the instrument at the other end had a distinctive ring that he was beginning to recognize.

"Hello! It's me."

She laughed.

"As if I didn't know."

"Well?"

"Well, yes."

"When?"

"This afternoon. She can't say exactly when."

"I understand."

"Anyway, not before three."

"Didn't she say anything else?"

"Only that she'd be there."

He wanted to shout, to wave his arms around in the booth, it was so marvelous. There must be no more drinking between now and three o'clock, he must get a grip on himself, keep calm. Besides, there was a lot to be done. For instance, he must buy flowers. Perhaps he ought to get friut as well. And he must do something about the room, try to cover up its miserable shabbiness.

"How much is it?"

All his triumph, all his happiness sounded in his voice, and three plasterers in white overalls fell silent and put down their drinks to stare at him.

Across the road were two large shopwindows, and in the half-light, near the cash desk, he saw the milky blur of a face crowned with black hair.

He was twenty-four years old.

Two days ago, in preparation for this great moment, he had given up his lodgings and moved into a room in the Hôtel Beauséjour, Rue Lepic.

"Anything wrong?"

He made a sign to Leduc that he was not to worry, and, with an effort, forced the glass between his lips to finish his drink.

He felt as though his face were no longer a part of him, as though his features, hard and set, no longer reflected his emotions. Even his eyes were expressionless, fixed in a stupefied stare.

"Don't you feel well?"

The change in his appearance must have been striking for Arthur to notice it. Arthur was looking pretty odd himself, for that matter, shocked and frightened, without a trace of his habitual flippancy.

"What's wrong?"

Without stopping to think, without consciously intending to put on an act, he set down his glass and put his hand on his chest.

"A spasm," he murmured.

"Is it your heart?"

"I think so. It's not the first time."

He could hear his voice as though it belonged to someone else, the voice of a dying man, and he tried to look away from the door.

"Do you want me to call your wife?"

"No. Don't say anything to her."

Had Arthur known what was going on, in the old days? It had never worried him. He must have overheard some of the telephone calls. Mariette was not the woman to keep anything from her husband.

"What do you feel, exactly?"

"It's hard to describe. It will pass."

To tell the truth, it was not an attack. He wished it had been. He wished he could be really ill. It would not be difficult, feeling as he did, to make them believe that he was. He had only to let go of himself, he thought, and he would drop to the floor like a dead man, oblivious of everything. Then they would send for Dr. Maresco, who would bend down to examine him.

Leduc, watching him in silence, did not look as if he knew. Perhaps there was nothing to know.

"It's getting easier."

"Have a drink."

He certainly felt like drinking, filling his glass with vermouth, gulping down everything he could lay hands on until he was too drunk to think. This had only happened to him once in his life, when he was twenty-two and had not yet met Louise. The next day he had felt like death.

"Do you want me to open the window?"

"No. And remember, say nothing to them."

The kitchen door was the first to open. Fernande asked in surprise:

"Where is madame?"

He jerked his chin in the direction of the bedroom.

"Dinner is ready. Shall I serve the soup?"

His wife and Mariette came in, and there was no change in Louise. She looked inquiringly at the girl.

Mariette seemed more lighthearted. She looked relieved.

"I was asking whether I should serve the soup."

"Yes, of course."

Only then did she turn to her husband. She frowned.

"Anything wrong?"

"It's nothing."

"Don't you feel well?"

"I'm all right now."

"Was it an attack?"

"I don't think so. I felt a bit groggy. It was probably the vermouth."

Why was Mariette looking at her husband like that? For reassurance? Yet she seemed anything but reassured.

"Shall we go to the table?" Louise said absently.

She kept looking at Etienne.

It was a very grave look, not just a passing ripple of anxiety; indeed, anxiety was the wrong word. It was the look of a woman confronted with a problem, and considering it soberly and calmly.

As if to prove it, she asked him no more questions, did not inquire further into his symptoms, but confined herself to quick glances, while, at the same time, ladling out the soup, as she always did.

"Wouldn't it be better if he went back to bed?" Mariette suggested.

"No," Louise said, as though she realized that it would do no good.

"What I do," Arthur said facetiously, to break the silence, "when I feel a cold coming on, is to empty a bottle of rum, and I tell Mariette . . ."

The words reverberated meaninglessly in Etienne's head. He was eating mechanically and staring at the others as though he had never seen them before.

The dinner dragged on in this way, and he scarcely knew what he had eaten. He had the impression that the air surrounding him was a solid yellowish backdrop against which all four of them stood out, like figures against the canvas in an old painting.

He was still conscious of his wife's glances, of Fernande's comings and goings, of her pale-blue blouse and white apron. He could not think now. He was incapable of thought. It was impossible in public.

Later, tomorrow, the next day, or the day after, he would have time to fit his fragmentary impressions together and, little by little, reconstruct an exact picture of the truth. As late as possible. Because the truth would be terrible.

Two or three times, he asked himself whether there was not still time to evade the issue. At such moments, he looked at Louise across the table and longed, in spite of the Leducs, to hold out his hand to her, so that she might take it in hers, thus sealing a kind of pact, that life would go on for the two of them and no questions would ever arise between them.

Might not this be possible? Had they not succeeded in keeping silent for fifteen years?

"Shall we two play against the women?" Leduc suggested, impatient to get down to the game of *belote*.

Etienne smelled the aroma of the *marc de bourgogne* being

poured into the glasses, as on every other Thursday, and all four stood waiting, while Fernande cleared the table and covered it with a green baize cloth.

"If we're playing against the men, we've won before we begin!" exclaimed Mariette, powdering her nose.

And, glancing at Etienne:

"You look just like one of those stuffed dummies at the fair that get balls thrown at them."

It was true, and he was well aware of it. It was the hardest thing in the world for him to draw back his lips in something that might pass for a smile; and, just at that moment, Louise's thoughtful eyes fixed on him.

Did she know that he was frightened?

4

Arthur Leduc suggested, not very hopefully:

"What about one last game for five hundred points?"

And Mariette, who was already standing up, tugging at her girdle through her dress, signaled to him to leave well enough alone, and said:

"Not tonight. Etienne is tired."

The men had won—Leduc always won, whoever his partner happened to be. He spent most days playing *belote* in brasseries in the neighborhood of Avenue Junot.

He sometimes introduced himself to people, with a queer light in his gray eyes, as "Arthur Leduc, Frenchman, vaccinated, aged 48, *belote* champion of the Eighteenth Arrondissement."

Once, some years back, he really had won the *belote* championship, which was contested in the various cafés of Montmartre.

Etienne and he had never exchanged confidences, and

Leduc, with his ceaseless flow of facetious talk, never said anything revealing about himself.

He was the son of a lawyer from Angoulême, who had sent him to Paris to study law. He had attended the university for two or three years, and then decided to try his luck as a ballad singer in the Montmartre cabarets.

He did not like to be reminded of this period of his life. He had stuck to it for a long time, breaking with his family, and dragging on in miserable poverty, before finally facing the fact that he had no talent.

He was already living with Mariette, who was little more than a child then, and who had left home to be with him. It was not until years later, when they were, at long last, married, that their parents forgave them and saw them from time to time.

It was Mariette who sometimes laughingly referred to those early days, when they were driven to rummaging in garbage cans, and, not having the price of a room, to sleeping back to back in station waiting rooms.

Arthur had worked in the advertising department of a newspaper. When it closed down, he persuaded himself that he had a talent for painting, and they had taken a studio near the Sacré-Coeur. Had he any illusions left? After a long succession of different jobs, he was now an insurance agent, in a halfhearted way, trailing from one Montmartre café to another.

Mariette kept the pot boiling. She had opened a hat shop on Avenue Junot, which, after a long struggle, had done well, and now, at the height of the season, she was able to keep four or five girls busy in the workroom.

The idea of reproaching her husband, of attempting to alter

his character or his way of life, had never occurred to her. She loved him as he was. One had only to see her the minute they set foot in the street, clutching his arm and struggling to keep up with his stride.

Much to his own surprise, Etienne had not made a slip all evening.

Gradually, he had become absorbed in the game, not because he found it interesting or attached any importance to it, but simply because it was a way of making time stand still, like those blank hours spent in a dentist's waiting room, before the sudden and startling moment of waking to the realization that one's own turn has come.

Louise, on the other hand, usually so self-assured, had once or twice seemed so preoccupied that Mariette had signaled to her to pull herself together.

What was it that had passed between them in the bedroom? What could they have had to say to each other that was so very urgent?

In a few minutes the Leducs would be gone. They were already exchanging the usual last-minute commonplaces. While Louise put the cards back in the drawer where they were kept, Mariette went to fetch her coat, and her husband uncoiled his bulky frame and lit a cigarette.

Louise and Etienne would be left alone. One of them would bolt the door, and they would both go into the bedroom, with the fairground illuminations making kaleidoscopic patterns on the walls.

He was suddenly panic-stricken. If he had known how, he would have kept their guests from leaving. He knew that nothing would happen, nothing could happen. There would just be the two of them, shut in together, spying on each other.

"See you next Thursday!" Mariette called out with forced gaiety. "Get better soon, Etienne!"

He smiled, much as Arthur Leduc smiled when he was introducing himself as *belote* champion. It seemed so strange to him to hear talk of another Thursday. Would it be possible for them to get that far, perhaps even to drag on from week to week, from stage to stage?

How long would it take?

What struck him most, and touched him deeply, was Leduc's handshake. The two women, framed in the doorway, had their backs to them. Instead of shaking hands casually, as he usually did, Arthur pressed Etienne's hand and held it in his grip for several seconds, without looking at him. It was as though he were trying to convey a message.

What message? Did he, too, know? Had he always known?

"See you Thursday," he said, in his turn.

Then, reverting to his waggish manner, he turned to Louise:

"Good night, boss!"

The staircase and the elevator, on its way to an upper floor, were very dimly lit, and the walls, neglected by the landlords for thirty years, had the mottled look of old churches.

"Good night," they said again.

"Good night."

The other two started down the stairs. In a moment, they would call out "Door, please!" to the concierge; the door would open, and they would be out in the cool evening air, surrounded by the lights and noises of the fair; Mariette's hand would grope for her husband's arm, while, on the landing of the mezzanine, Etienne and Louise stood in front of the gaping door of their apartment.

What would the Leducs say to each other, out there? Would they stop for a final drink on the terrace of the Cyrano bar, and talk over their evening, at the same time idly watching the antics of the prostitutes?

"Are you coming in?" Louise asked, almost in a whisper.

The way she said it sounded odd to him, and he gave her a swift look, wondering how she would behave, now that they were left to themselves.

He followed her inside, and into the dining room, knowing that, before going to bed, she would put the bottles back in the sideboard, take the dirty glasses into the kitchen, and rinse them, so that the apartment would not smell of drink in the morning.

She did it all, exactly as she had always done, moving in the same way, with the same impassive expression, but still, there was a difference. It was as though they had lost contact, not only with each other, but with the things around them, and she was making no attempt to re-establish it.

"Shall we go to bed?"

Her voice had an unfamiliar ring. For an instant, as they were going toward the bedroom, and she turned around, bringing him up short, he had the impression that, because he had been behind her so that she could not see what he was doing, she had given a tiny shudder of fear.

That she turned on the light to dispel the shadows, and then let down her hair before taking off her dress, was also significant.

Only the night before, it had been possible for them. Could it still happen?

It embarrassed him to undress in front of her. He turned his back to put on his pajama trousers. Not daring to close the bathroom door, he nevertheless half shut it as he went in.

"Aren't you going to take your temperature?"

"No."

"Well, I don't suppose you have one."

"Probably not."

"How's your cold?"

"Better, I think."

"Your nose wasn't running much while we were playing cards."

It was true, though he had not realized it. He had not had to go for a clean handkerchief. His nose seemed less inflamed, and the stiffness in his neck was almost gone.

When he came out of the bathroom and she went in, he avoided looking at her, feeling ill at ease when he heard sounds that evoked an intimate picture.

"Shall I put out the light?"

"If you like."

Just as she was switching it off, he changed his mind.

"I'd better have a sleeping pill."

It was very rarely indeed that either of them took a sleeping pill; once in a blue moon, for a raging toothache, or after having had too much coffee.

"Don't you think you'll be able to get to sleep?"

She did not pursue it, but went into the bathroom, and came back with a white tablet and a glass of water. He was already lying down in bed. She stood very close to him in her nightgown, and all he could see was her outline, from the waist down. Her nightgown brushed his cheek as she bent down.

Had he any hope left? He no longer knew. He raised himself on one elbow, took the glass, and, only after he had drunk from it, raised his eyes. She was looking him up and down, calmly as ever, but with unusual thoughtfulness.

After putting out the light, she got into bed and settled

herself under the covers. He wondered whether she would go through the familiar ritual. He waited, holding his breath. She hesitated—he was sure of it—then moved toward him until her face was almost against his. He felt the warmth of her breath, as she whispered:

"Good night, Etienne."

Without having to grope for them, her lips touched his, lightly, with no eagerness, but with no reluctance, either.

"Good night, Louise."

Ordinarily, when they were both settled for the night, they would whisper once more, after a moment of silence:

"Good night, Louise."

"Good night, Etienne."

With a feeling of anguish, he said it. She replied. And then silence filled the room.

For a long time, he lay there with his eyes open, staring at the window lit up from outside, wondering whether the sleeping pill would have any effect. He did not want to think. Not yet. He was not ready. He knew that once he started, it would be long and painful, with no hope of turning back.

He kept repeating to himself words that had no meaning, as, when he was a child, he used to mumble to himself, after being punished by his mother:

"It's not possible. She can't be as wicked as that. She'll realize what she's done, and then she'll be sorry."

Tonight, too, he said:

"It's not possible."

Some people outside were chasing one another and colliding in bumper cars, others were walking along, peacefully talking of their own affairs.

Louise was not asleep. He was certain that she was not

asleep. Perhaps she, too, was lying with her eyes open, watching the lights reflected on the bathroom door.

He could not hear her breathing. She was lying perfectly still, so still that, after a time, he longed to put out his hand and touch her, to make sure that she was alive.

He dared not do it.

He did not hold anything against her, he bore her no ill will. Was it really not possible to ask her straight out? Perhaps he need not even put it in so many words. In the darkness that enfolded them both, could he not just murmur:

"Tell me, Louise, is it *yes?*"

She would understand. He was sure of it. Only it would be impossible for her to reply:

"It is *yes.*"

Because if she did, what would be the outcome?

There was no solution. She could not say it. It was pointless to ask the question.

She, too, must be burning to say:

"Have you guessed?"

At the very thought, sweat broke out on his forehead. He, too, would have found it impossible to reply.

He was very hot. He was going to perspire again, as he had done the night before. He was clammy from head to foot already. A bitter taste came into his mouth, the taste of the sleeping tablet.

Why had Arthur Leduc pressed his hand so insistently? To encourage him? Could Arthur see any solution? Or was it simply that he had wanted to show his sympathy?

Perhaps it would do him good to talk to Leduc. He had never confided in anyone. In fact, he now realized, he had never had a real friend. Even at school. Even as a young man, before his military service, when he had worked in a bank at

Lyons. And his parents had never known what he was thinking.

Not only had he had no friends, he had also had no mistresses in the generally accepted sense of the word.

Most of his companions used to go out with the same girl for weeks or months on end, persuading themselves that they were in love; behaving, at any rate, as though the girls meant something to them.

Why had this not happened to him? He had tried, often. He had taken girls to the movies, and walked with them beside the Rhône, or out in the country. He had got as far as a few clumsy caresses. But, after that, there were things that must be said, and he had no inclination to say them.

He was conscious of their small failings, their pathetic little worries, and he felt more pity than desire for them.

When his need was unbearable, he would accost a prostitute, always at the same crossroads, because, in that relationship, there was no need for talk.

He had never walked arm in arm with a girl who was both friend and lover, never, like other men out with their girls, burst out laughing over nothing at all. And when, after his military service, he had come to Paris, he had sometimes wandered about for hours at night, feeling sick at heart whenever he saw the shadow of a man and a woman on a window shade.

Louise made an almost imperceptible movement, and he started, with a rush of hope, although he knew that there was nothing to hope for. She, too, must be intent on listening to his breathing. Was she unhappy? Did she feel any pity for him?

Often in the course of nearly sixteen years, he had looked at her furtively, with a question on his lips. He was convinced that she was aware of it, that she dreaded that question.

They needed each other so much! Did she not realize that?

His legs felt heavy under the sheet. His body was growing numb. It was not thoughts that were passing through his head, but images, not all of which were very distinct.

For instance, there was the image of the man who had lain for so long in this very room. Not in the same bed. Before their marriage, Louise had refurnished the apartment, and sent the old furniture to the auction rooms.

He could see her still, at the cashier's desk, leaning toward the iron staircase to listen. She was saying, in her impersonal businesswoman's voice:

"If you'll come this way . . ."

Was it conceivable that the stockman had noticed nothing? More often than not he was there, arranging the goods on the shelves. Sometimes, she took the trouble to send him to the stockroom, but she could not do this on every occasion.

There was a counter at the back, which could not be seen from Monsieur Théo's glass-walled printing office. It was toward this that she guided him: her hips full and rounded even then, the nape of her neck just as it was now, white and a little plump, against her black hair.

She would turn around, to make sure that they were completely screened from Monsieur Charles by the staircase, and always, at the same time, glance quickly toward the shop-windows.

Then, as if it were the most natural thing in the world, as it was when Mariette took her husband's arm, she would throw her arms around his neck and press her mouth against his.

It was over in an instant.

"We stock a file I'd like you to see. I think it might interest you."

Was the man up there listening? Had he, too, been suspiciously alert to every sound in the shop?

She whispered in his ear:

"I'll try to slip out tomorrow morning, about nine."

Sometimes she added:

"It won't be long now!"

So as to be with him in his hotel room on Rue Lepic, where he spent hours sitting on the edge of the bed waiting for her, she was forever having to invent new subterfuges.

Even in those days, it was she who ran the business. On the pretext that the maid was incapable of doing the shopping, she sometimes managed to get away in the morning. Rue Lepic was cluttered up with small barrows. There was a stream of housewives going up the street, and another going down it. The hotel chambermaid was doing the rooms, and most of the doors were standing open.

Often, Louise had to step over buckets and brooms.

She gave him one first kiss, then at once tore herself away from him, and stripped off her dress and underclothes, eager to show herself naked to him, exulting in her power.

"Do you love me?"

"Yes."

"Are you happy?"

Even if she could only spare him ten minutes, she would undress completely, her eyes full of joy and pride.

"Will you walk past the shop?"

"Yes."

"About what time?"

In those days, he was working for Southwestern Paper Mills. Their chief representative in Paris had assigned him to the Right Bank. It was as a commercial traveler that he had walked into the shop on Boulevard de Clichy one morning, carrying a heavy case of samples, in the humble and ingratiating manner of a beggar.

He could still remember that he had spoken first to a man in a brownish overall, and that, because of the name over the door, he had said:

"Monsieur Birard?"

Monsieur Charles had replied:

"I'll call Madame Gatin."

He had gone into the glass-walled printing office, where there was a young woman in black talking to a man.

The first glance she had given him had been from behind this wall of glass that divided the printing office from the shop. He had seen her lips move as she said something to the stockman.

"Madame Gatin will see you in a moment."

That was her first husband's name, Guillaume Gatin.

It was a hot July morning. A municipal street-sprinkling truck was moving slowly along the boulevard. The shop door was standing open.

She had finished talking to Monsieur Théo, and was at last moving toward him. He had been wearing a straw hat that day, and had put it down on top of the stack of files. It was quite a long way from the printing office to the cashier's desk, as the shop extended to the back of the building, and, all the time she was walking toward him, he never took his eyes off her.

"I beg your pardon..." he stammered, as she came up to him.

For what? He had no idea. He was agitated, and he sensed her awareness of it.

"I'm the new representative of Southwestern Paper Mills. You've dealt with them for a long time, I believe."

They had not sat down, but stood side by side at one of the counters, where Etienne had spread out his samples, and

Louise had leaned forward on her elbows, so close to him that he could feel the warmth of her body.

"When will you be coming again?"

"Next week, same day, if you can let me have your order then."

She had said simply, "Do come!," holding out her hand, and looking into his eyes.

"You seemed so very young and so upset!" she had explained later.

On his second visit, after he had taken her order, she had asked him upstairs for a drink.

"That's the way they do it in big business, isn't it?"

For the first time, he had started up the iron staircase, and had been surprised, when he got to the top, to find that it led into a bedroom.

"Please forgive me for bringing you this way, but it's shorter than going through the archway."

He remembered nothing of the maid but her apron. He had not noticed her face.

"Two glasses, Julie," Louise had said to her.

And to him:

"Would you prefer a long drink?"

"I'll have whatever you're having."

The dining-room windows were open, and there was a hot breeze, with fitful currents of cooler air.

He never discovered whether she had brought him upstairs deliberately, or whether she had entertained other salesmen there before him. He had never dared to ask her.

After sixteen years, the smell of the vermouth and its color in the glasses came back to him, and he remembered that, as she drank, he had noticed the tiny beads of moisture on her upper lip.

"Are you married, Monsieur Lomel?"

"No, madame."

"You're very young, aren't you?"

"I'm twenty-four."

At that time, he did not know Louise's age. She was just thirty.

"Have you been in Paris long?"

He had not yet learned to interpret the slight tremor of her lip. He made some incoherent reply, and, when he put out his hand to pick up his glass, it touched hers. He felt moist fingers interlaced with his. He looked into her eyes and was held by them. Then suddenly, he was holding her, not knowing whether it was he who had drawn her to him, or she who had thrown herself into his arms.

Why, during that first kiss, had he felt his eyes filling with tears?

He had a feeling of coming home at last. There was a warm body pressed against his, and he could not bring himself to release it. He was already afraid of losing her.

They did not notice the telephone ringing downstairs. Monsieur Charles called out from the bottom of the stairs.

"Are you there, madame? It's Labouchère's wanting to speak to you."

They went down, one behind the other, and Etienne felt unsteady on the narrow staircase.

As he lay in bed now, tears ran down his cheeks.

He wept silently, without a single sob.

"Are you asleep?" whispered Louise.

His failure to reply was not deliberate. He was numb, as though there were layers of some intangible substance between him and reality.

He had returned often to Boulevard de Clichy, but because

74

of the staff, Louise could not always take him upstairs. It was then that they went to the dark corner at the back of the shop; though even this was only possible when Monsieur Charles happened to be in the right place, screened from view by the staircase.

A month after their first meeting, he had taken her, savagely, almost despairingly, on the bed on the first floor, and afterward they had stared at each other wildly, not knowing whether it was love or hate that was in their eyes.

Had she felt resentful afterward? Had he disappointed her? For weeks, she had spoken to him coldly, every time he telephoned.

He had been afraid to go into the shop, which he had to pass several times a day. In the end, it was she who had come to the door and called him in.

Did she, too, sometimes look back on this period of their life?

Once, and once only, he had met her husband. It was in the autumn. He had caught sight of a corpulent man of about forty, with a brown mustache, standing in front of one of the counters, and, as he was wearing a fawn overcoat and a hat, Etienne had mistaken him for a customer.

She had introduced them to each other.

"My husband. Monsieur Lomel, the Southwestern Paper Mills representative."

"Pleased to meet you."

She had remained perfectly self-possessed.

"My husband calls on the customers," she had explained later. "When we were married, after my father died, I was just seventeen, and I didn't know anything about business."

He had begged to be allowed to see her again, alone, and it was then that he had made up his mind to take a room on

Rue Lepic. Before that, he had lived in furnished lodgings on Rue Lafayette, not far from the Gare du Nord.

"You'd better not be seen in the shop too often. It would be better if you didn't ring me up here any more, either. I can't always be sure of taking the call."

She had told him about Mariette, who was to be their go-between.

"I went to school with her. She's the only friend I've got. I don't in the least mind her knowing."

Between himself and this woman on the telephone whom he had never seen, there had grown up a kind of intimacy, the intimacy of conspirators.

"It's you again!" she would exclaim, recognizing his voice. "What if I say I don't have any message for you?"

"Please don't make fun of me."

"Right. Don't worry, my dear. If you're good, she'll be with you between three and four. Will you be in?"

He would sooner have resigned from Southwestern Paper Mills, and worked all night unloading vegetables in Les Halles, than have missed a single one of their meetings. The room on Rue Lepic had no redeeming feature; it was not even very clean, but Louise did not seem to notice. He spent hours waiting for her, and, after her visits, he had to rush all over the place to make up for lost time.

Sometime between Christmas and New Year's Day, Louise had announced:

"Next week, I may have a big surprise for you."

He had implored her so insistently to tell him what it was, that at last she had given way.

"My sister-in-law in La Rochelle is ill. There isn't much hope that she'll recover. If she dies, my husband will have to go to the funeral."

The sister-in-law had died, and they had two nights to themselves, which they spent in the little hotel room.

On the last morning, as she dressed, her face was unusually hard.

"Do you think you really love me?"

"I know I do."

"Enough to spend your whole life with me?"

It seemed to him patently obvious.

"Give yourself time to think. Don't answer now."

"But . . ."

"Next time I come, tell me truthfully whether you're willing to marry me."

She left without kissing him. For the next three days, every time he telephoned Mariette, she said:

"She's not free today, my dear."

She was obviously sorry for him.

"Why not?"

"How should I know? Maybe her husband is home with the flu!"

"Is that it?"

"It's just a guess. Unless it's that she just doesn't feel like seeing you."

When he saw her again, it was half past nine in the morning. It was very cold, and the light was as clear as the sky. There were braziers burning in the street, and the women at the strawberry stalls were taking turns warming their hands at them.

Instead of kissing him at once, Louise, her face impassive, had stopped in the doorway and murmured:

"What have you decided?"

"You know there's nothing I want more than to marry you."

"And you will?"

Gently she pushed him away from her.

"Of course. I love you. I love you with all my strength, with . . ."

"Oh, come! No, not that . . ."

Her long kiss left him breathless.

"What is it?" he said anxiously, seeing her move toward the door.

"I'm going."

"But . . ."

"Not today. You mustn't try to see me for the next few days."

Was she asleep at last? Was she remembering, too?

The fairground music had stopped. There were fewer people around, and the sound of their footsteps on the sidewalk was more resonant.

"*I said to him straight out: 'What kind of a fool do you take me for?'* " said a voice, slurred with drink.

"*And what did he say to that?*"

The voices faded as the speakers approached Place Blanche.

From the day Louise had come back, and for the following week, there had been a subtle difference in their relationship. Perhaps he had misinterpreted her attitude. She seemed calmer, more thoughtful, yet she made love with heightened intensity.

Was it that they now regarded themselves as man and wife?

"Are you certain you'll never get tired of me?"

He protested. She cut him short.

"Have you ever stopped to think that I'm almost an old woman?"

The spring passed. It was summer, and he noticed that the fair was on as he went into the shop one afternoon. Once a month, he paid an official visit as the representative of Southwestern Paper Mills.

He did not at first understand the sign she made to him from the cashier's desk, and he wondered why she did not take him to their corner at the back of the shop.

"I was just making out my order."

It was true. She finished it there and then, and pointed up the stairs.

As she was seeing him to the door, he whispered:

"Your husband?"

She nodded.

"Is he ill?"

She nodded again. Then, raising her voice, she said:

"Good-by, Monsieur Lomel. Please see to it that the order is delivered as soon as possible."

He was in turmoil the whole evening. He could not wait to talk to her, to ply her with questions. When he telephoned Mariette, she said:

"I'm afraid you'll have to be patient, my dear."

"Is her husband ill?"

"You know?"

After a pause, he had stammered:

"Is it serious?"

She had replied with forced lightness, as though she found the subject distasteful:

"I believe so."

In the next fortnight, he saw Louise only twice. The first time she was in and out like a gust of wind.

"I must get back right away. I only came out to see to an order."

He opened his mouth, but she would not let him speak.

"No! I can't discuss that now."

It was not until she was in the doorway that she asked him, in an almost hostile tone:

"Do you love me?"

She asked him the same question when she came the next time, while they were in each other's arms, her body pressed against his with a kind of predatory desperation, as though she were bent on destroying him.

"If ever you tried to get out of loving me . . ."

One morning, as he was turning onto Boulevard de Clichy, he received a shock. The shutters were down over the windows of the stationer's shop, and posted on the door was a notice announcing a death in the house. The concierge, on the porch, was talking to a couple of neighbors, explaining what had happened, no doubt.

He was so confused that he found himself sitting in a bus without the least idea of where he was going.

He called on a few customers, feeling as though he were groping about in thick and icy fog. A dozen times, passing some bar or other, he was on the point of going in to telephone Mariette.

What could he say to her?

At about midday, he called in to his hotel to see if there was a message for him. There was nothing. When he got back from work, there was still no message, and he spent the evening lying on his bed, staring at the ceiling.

For three days, he had no contact whatsoever either with Louise or with Mariette, and, on the morning of the funeral, he stood on the corner of Place Blanche, hidden behind a newspaper stand, seeing the black draperies over the door, and the groups of people gathering under the trees.

He saw the coffin go by. He saw Louise, too, in deep mourning, her face hidden behind her veil, getting into the first car, with a plump little woman, and a man who seemed ill at ease.

They were Mariette and her husband, whom at that time he had not met.

He waited until four o'clock in the afternoon before telephoning from the bar on the corner. The sky was overcast. There were lights on in the houses. The shutters were still down over the shop front, but the mezzanine windows were lit up.

The sound of the telephone bell ringing in the apartment troubled him. He had to wait a long time. It was Mariette who answered.

"Could I speak to Louise?"

"I'll go and see."

Mariette did not seem to recognize his voice. He heard a murmur of voices. Someone picked up the handset.

"Is that you?" Louise asked.

"Yes."

He was at a loss for words; he had forgotten what he had intended to say to her.

Foolishly, he said:

"How are you?"

"I'm well."

There was a silence. He was afraid that they had been cut off. Then he heard Louise's voice again. She sounded worried.

"And you?"

"I'm longing to see you."

"Sure?"

"Yes."

She seemed reluctant to let him come right away. Mariette and Arthur must have stayed to keep her company after the funeral.

"Would you mind terribly waiting till tomorrow?"

"No, if that's what you'd prefer."

"It would be wiser, I think. Call me tomorrow."

Suddenly, out of the depths of his drugged torpor, a tiny phrase rang in his ears as though it were being spoken at that very moment:

"Now, it's safe."

And, shaken by a sort of convulsion, he dug his nails into the palms of his hands to keep himself from screaming.

Louise touched him lightly on the thigh to make sure that he was asleep, and he managed, somehow or other, to keep perfectly still.

It was as though he were afraid of confronting the realities of a new day. With eyes closed, he listened to the rain splashing on the windows, and dripping from the trees in the boulevard. He was careful not to make the smallest movement, to lie still as he had lain in sleep, doubled up like a child in its mother's womb. He did not even attempt to free his hand, which was entangled in the sheet. He had a strange feeling that, by remaining motionless, he was somehow warding off his fate.

At the same time, his mind and senses were alert, and he could tell, from the noises outside, the rumbling of buses and delivery vans, that the day had begun.

There was no sound yet from the shop. Cautiously, like an animal exploring new ground, he slid his foot sideways between the sheets, and encountered nothing but cool linen.

Louise was up. She was not in the bathroom. He was straining to discover where she was, when he heard the chink of a cup and saucer behind the dining-room door. This tiny sound was followed by whispering, from which he gathered that his wife was having breakfast, and giving instructions to the maid.

He could still feel the effects of last night's sedative. His tongue was coated, and his whole body voluptuously relaxed. It was a long time before he could rouse himself to turn his head and half open his eyes, to look at the alarm clock and see the time. The hands stood at half past eight.

He had no intention of getting up yet, and, feeling for the imprint of his body in the bed, he took pains to settle back, as best he could, into exactly the same position as before. It was raining heavily, in a steady downpour. No doubt pools were collecting on the canvas awnings of the fairground booths.

A chair scraped. The door opened. Though he did not hear the handle turn, he felt a slight draft, and knew that his wife must be looking at him through the crack. He lay stiller than ever, drawing deep, even breaths, so as to seem asleep.

Now she came forward on tiptoe, pausing at every step. He was conscious of a shadow between him and the window. She watched him in silence. He felt a pricking in his right eyelid, and it needed all his strength to keep it from twitching and giving him away.

Time seemed to pass slowly. He was aware of a faint smell of soap, of the freshness of Louise's person. She retreated so softly that she had reached the door before the creak of a shoe told him that she had moved.

She went into the kitchen to speak to Fernande, and their two voices reminded him of the murmur of the confessional. It must have been two or three minutes to nine, as usual, when she went down the iron staircase, pausing at each step. When he heard the ring of her feet on the tiled floor of the shop, he was able at last to relax his cramped muscles.

He would have preferred, that day, to have no contact with

any human being, not even with the people in the street, through the glass rectangle of the window. He wanted to shut himself in behind double-locked doors, to go to ground, like an animal. But there was no place that he could really call his own. This room was not his; the daily routine starting up downstairs owed nothing to his presence. It had gone on in the same way long before he had set foot in the house.

Monsieur Charles was raising the shutters, and this reminded him that the stockman never spoke to him unless he had to. As far back as he could remember, they had never exchanged a superfluous word, never, for instance, remarked to each other, as strangers do, that the weather was fine, or that it was raining, or that the bus was late.

He did not want his wife coming up and asking how he was, and he moved toward the bathroom in his bare feet, as cautiously as she had moved toward him. He did not look well, he thought. He was probably imagining things, but for some time now it had seemed to him that his growth of beard was heavier than it used to be; he had heard it said that the beards of the dead grew at a surprising rate in the first few hours.

The telephone at the cashier's desk rang as he was putting on his brown wool dressing gown, which made him look like a monk. He stood still at the head of the iron staircase. Louise was speaking softly, for fear of waking him.

"Hello . . . Yes . . . Is that you? . . . I don't know. . . . He's still asleep."

It must be Mariette, asking after his health. And what was she talking about after that, with Louise saying nothing but "Yes . . . Yes . . . Yes . . . Yes . . ." almost at regular intervals?

He counted seventeen "yesses" before she said at last: "I'll tell him. Good-by."

He stayed where he was for a moment to make sure that she was not coming upstairs, then went into the kitchen. Fernande, hearing him behind her, gave a start.

"You frightened me."

"I'd like a cup of coffee."

Was it because she, too, thought he looked ill that she was staring at him like that?

"Don't you want your breakfast?"

"No."

"I'll bring you your coffee in the dining room."

"Give me a cup here."

He waited for the coffee to be poured, put sugar in it, took the cup into the bedroom, and sat in the armchair near the window. In this sort of weather, the showmen scarcely set foot outside their caravans, and he could imagine them with their families, packed into the tiny space, like rabbits in a warren.

Half-consciously, he envied them.

A little later, a conversation over the speaking tube between Louise and Fernande brought a faint smile to his lips. From where he was sitting, he could hear the two voices, so different in tone and pitch, the one coming from the foot of the stairs, the other from behind the kitchen door.

Louise spoke softly:

"Can you hear me, Fernande?"

Fernande, not attempting to keep her voice down, replied: "Yes, madame."

"Is monsieur still asleep?"

"No, madame. He has just been in to fetch his coffee."

He knew that, downstairs, his wife was hesitating, staring at nothing, and asking herself what she ought to do. The situation was even more difficult for her than for him. She must know that he knew, and even supposing that she was not quite sure, the uncertainty would be even more distressing for her.

It was for Etienne's benefit that she began talking to Monsieur Charles, in her everyday voice, giving him instructions about outstanding orders, which were probably quite unnecessary. She was trying to restore the rhythm of daily life, by drawing on the vocabulary of the business and invoking the familiar names of her customers.

After that, there was silence, a new, empty silence. At last, he heard the vibration of the first step of the iron staircase, then Louise's tread, resolute now, as she came quickly up the stairs.

"Are you up?"

The sight of him, in his dressing gown, with his hair uncombed, was a shock to her. She had not expected to find him there in the armchair, with his back to the light.

"Aren't you going to have your breakfast?"

"I'm not hungry."

Etienne's voice sounded unfamiliar, toneless, and flat. It was not intentional. He had not meant to frighten her, but he was not altogether displeased to see her put out of countenance.

"Don't you feel well?"

"I'm much better."

"What about your cold?"

"It's almost gone."

He added, almost as a challenge:

"I may go out later."

"It would be stupid to go out in this downpour, after three days in bed."

"I'll see, this afternoon."

"Aren't you going back to bed?"

"No."

"Will you stay where you are?"

"I think I will."

She did not force the thermometer routine on him. She wanted to humor him, and it must be frustrating for her not to be able to see his face clearly, only an outline against the light, so that she could not study his expression.

"Mariette telephoned to ask after you."

He did not say that he knew. He said nothing.

"She says she hopes you'll soon be well."

Could she see the corner of his mouth twitching in a mirthless smile?

"Are you going to take your bath?"

"Not now."

If it interfered with the housework, it was just too bad. He did not feel like a bath. He did not feel like shaving, either.

"I'll have to go back to the shop."

"Yes."

Finally, as if to prove that today was not so very different from any other, she came close to him and, bending down, kissed him on the forehead.

"If you need anything, call me. Wouldn't you like me to have the papers sent up?"

"No."

Was this what it had been like, in the old days, with the other one? Guillaume Gatin had spent months in this same room, looking out of the windows at the same view, listening to the same noises from downstairs. Etienne remembered that then, when Louise came to him on Rue Lepic, she took a roundabout way, so as not to be seen crossing the boulevard from the house.

It was not the same armchair. All the furniture had been

changed. But there certainly had been an armchair just there.

"See you later."

"See you later," he repeated after her.

His cold really was better. There was nothing to prevent his going out if he felt like it. Only, he did not feel like it. He did not feel like anything. He was exhausted in mind and body. He did not have the strength to move, or read; he did not have the strength even to think.

Later in the morning, when he felt up to it, he would scribble some notes on the sheet hidden inside the covers of *Social Life in the Insect World*. To do this, he would have to get up from his chair. He did not call Fernande to ask for another cup of coffee, not so much because it was an effort, as because he preferred to wait until she finished her work in the dining room and came in to make the bed.

There was no denying that if he had made up his mind to walk out, he would have found it difficult to do so. The thought had never entered his head until this morning. It had struck him suddenly, and he was staggered by it.

Had Louise planned it deliberately? It was possible. He believed her capable of it, not in cold blood, but to bind him to her more securely, by depriving him of any life of his own.

At the time of their marriage, she had said nothing to him. In the weeks following, he had carried on his job with Southwestern Paper Mills, setting out in the morning and often not getting back until the evening, though he never failed to telephone three or four times a day.

One evening he had found her looking worried.

"I'll have to find someone," she said.

At first, he had not understood what she meant.

"I keep getting complaints. The customers resent it. They've got used to relying on a traveler."

She never referred directly to her first husband.

"What do you think?"

"What about?"

"I've been asking myself all day whether you should go on working for Southwestern Paper Mills, or whether it would be better for you to give it up and work for us."

She had said "*for us.*" It was a distortion of the facts. He had no stake in her business. It had seemed to him quite natural, on the eve of their marriage, to call on his wife's lawyer and sign a document waiving all rights in her property. When it was read over to him, he had not even troubled to listen.

"Think it over, Etienne. I don't want to influence you. Though, of course, I'd be happier if we were working together."

The only thing that held him back was the image of Guillaume Gatin, still clear in his memory, as he had looked when Etienne had seen him for the first and last time, standing at the counter in his fawn spring coat, with his hat on.

All the same, in their bedroom two hours later, he had said:

"I'll hand in my resignation at the end of the week."

He wanted to be as close as possible to her in all things. Had there been anything at the back of Louise's mind? There had never been any question of remuneration. When he needed money, he asked his wife for it. It had seemed the natural thing, as it was she who kept the accounts and ran the business.

There were times when the situation was embarrassing, when he wanted to give her a present, for instance, and he had to invent some pretext, and afterward confess to the deception.

The shop, the stock, the furniture, everything in the place, belonged to Louise, and at the age of forty, he had nothing that he could call his own. If he looked at the matter logically, even the few hundred-franc notes in his wallet were not really his property.

Again, his mouth twitched. It was almost a sneer. Sitting there in his corner, conscious of the bristles on his unshaven face, and watching Fernande turning the mattress, he had suddenly seen Louise in a new light. Was this the truth at last? Was that how others saw her? Had he been the only one to take a different view of her?

The maids, he suspected, found her hard and avaricious. The local tradesmen, he fancied, did, too. Her manner, when she spoke to them on the telephone, had made him feel uncomfortable more than once.

But what of old Monsieur Théo? Had he stayed with her all this time only out of loyalty to the memory of her father, who had been a friend to him as well as an employer?

And Monsieur Charles? Was he just a sheep, a complacent nonentity, too timid to look further afield?

Was it just a harmless joke, with no malice intended, when Arthur Leduc referred to Louise as "*the boss*"?

At other times, he called her "Juno."

What did people say of him? At school, where he had not attached himself to any group, his schoolmates had probably disliked him for his self-sufficiency. He remembered one of the masters interrupting a lesson to bark at him irritably, with a spiteful glint in his eye:

"*What are you mooning about this time, Lomel?*"

And his mother, when she was reproving him for something or other:

"Of course, you're not listening to a word I'm saying. You can't bring yourself to admit you're in the wrong. Your pride won't let you."

Proud, that was what they called him in the barracks, too, and in the various offices in which he had worked subsequently. His fellow workers had never treated him as one of them.

He had always been an outsider, and people mistrust outsiders, not bothering to ask themselves why.

Until his meeting with Louise.

He thought of himself as he had been the first time she took him up to the apartment for a glass of vermouth. He reddened a little; he was ashamed of the spiteful picture of her that he had just built up, as a kind of revenge.

She was speaking on the telephone downstairs. He listened to her level voice as she went through the items of an order.

Had he not been guilty, just now, of treachery toward her? Had his own conduct been any more creditable?

What, for instance, had people thought of him, of his actions and motives, when he had come to live in the house?

He seldom looked back on that period. He had lived through it in a fever, a sort of sick confusion of mind, which it was not pleasant to recall.

When he telephoned Louise, in the days following the funeral, it was not to arrange a meeting either at her home or in his room on Rue Lepic. It was just to keep in touch, to reassure himself.

Had she known that he would not force the pace?

"Louise?"

"Yes."

"How do you feel?"

"All right. A bit tired. And you?"

He talked of anything that came into his head, to keep her on the phone as long as he could. He did not know what was going to happen. It was up to her to decide.

On the fourth day, she had said:

"Listen, Etienne. I was wondering whether we couldn't manage to get away for a two-week holiday together. I could leave Monsieur Charles to look after the shop. If you can make it, meet me the day after tomorrow at the Gare de Lyon. We could get a train leaving at about five."

He had had to borrow money, and pawn his watch. That was in March. They had gone to Nice. In her black suit, white blouse, and tiny hat, she had seemed to him more fragile than when he had seen her last.

In the train they had scarcely spoken to each other. Next morning, when they stepped onto the platform in Nice, the sunshine was more dazzling than anything he had ever known. Outside the station, the air was full of the sweetish scent of mimosa. It was she who had chosen their hotel. It was on Promenade des Anglais, although some distance away from the great luxury hotels.

They had both registered under their own names, but had taken a double room.

He had supposed that there must be a time of waiting before they could be lovers again, but he had been wrong. At once, without waiting to unpack the luggage, with the sea glittering under their window, and a child in a red bathing suit playing in the sand on the beach, she had turned to him with a wild look and begun to tear off her clothes.

That morning, when it had seemed that their bodies were attuned only to pain and violence, she had looked deep into his eyes and, with her teeth clenched in a kind of fury, had asked him:

"Are you sure you love me?"

He had understood that all they had ever said to each other in the past counted for nothing, it was what was said now that mattered. He had known, too, that she was straining to detect any hesitation, any slight tremor in his voice.

"I love you."

"I'll never let you go, do you understand?"

Knowing everything, he had said yes, he understood.

During their two weeks together, they had not spoken to anyone, but lived a life apart like a wolf and a she-wolf in the forest, and they cared for nothing but each other and what they could see in each other's eyes.

She had waited until the last day to announce:

"By law, I have to wait ten months before I can marry again. I don't give a damn what people say. You're coming to live with me."

Later, she had asked him point-blank:

"Have you been baptized?"

"I was brought up as a Catholic."

"So was I. When the time comes, we'll be married in church."

She no longer went to Mass. Possibly, she did not believe in God. But she wanted him tied to her by the strongest possible bonds.

When they returned to Paris, he noticed that the bedroom had been completely refurnished, and that there was a new maid.

The dead man's clothes were gone from the wardrobes. The only thing left that had belonged to Guillaume Gatin was a broken pipe, which Etienne had come upon one day at the back of a drawer.

He had put it in his pocket, and, because he could not bring himself to throw it out with the rubbish, had found some pretext for going across the Seine that day, and had flung it into the water from the bridge.

The concierge had never accepted him as a member of the household, even after their marriage, which took place a year later; first the civil ceremony in the Town Hall of the Ninth Arrondissement, then the wedding in the Church of the Trinity, which was cool and empty. Whenever he went past the concierge's lodge, she stared at him contemptuously through the curtains, and she would speak only to Louise.

For a long time, he did not know the official cause of Guillaume Gatin's death. He could not ask his wife, or, indeed, anyone else.

Once or twice, for some minor ailment, they had called in Dr. Rivet, a man with a white beard and beetling eyebrows, and he, too, had stared at Etienne in an unpleasant way.

Many months later, standing at the open window, he had become aware of the concierge talking to a local woman on the sidewalk, and overheard their conversation.

Indeed, he had the feeling that the concierge knew that he was there, and was deliberately raising her voice for his benefit.

"Yes, indeed. No one would ever have guessed that the poor man had heart trouble. He was always so cheerful! And he would never go by without a friendly word."

Had she looked up at this point, to make sure that the window was open?

"The undertaker's man told me he was so thin when he died that, when they lifted him into the coffin, he weighed no more than a child of ten."

In their fifteen years together, he had never questioned his wife, and the notion that she might be tempted to confide in him had, more than once, made him sweat with fear.

In Paris, as in Nice, they had lived alone, entrenched in the heart of the teeming city, and only the Leducs, once a week, came to see them.

He had had an odd feeling when Louise had said to him, in front of them:

"There's no need to be so formal with them."

His joints felt stiff as he got up, took the Fabre from the shelf, and glanced through the notes on the sheet of paper. He added in pencil:

"Wednesday, 24th: Read.

"Thursday, 25th: Belote. Louise-Mariette talked.

"Friday, 26th: Mariette—telephone."

The notes were intelligible to him, but that was not enough. When he had the strength, he would write out a full statement, recording all the facts and dates.

It was too late to find anything out from Dr. Rivet—he had been dead two years. But Etienne would go and see the doctor on Avenue des Ternes again, and this time, he would ask specific questions.

He did not want to die. But neither did he want to leave Louise. She was all he had in the world.

Had she not begged him never to leave her?

He could hear her moving downstairs, and the mere sound of her footsteps was comforting.

He no longer wanted to go out of the house, to lose touch with her.

Had the pattern of events been the same for Guillaume?

He must try to recall the time sequence. His lips moved soundlessly as he counted the months.

Guillaume had been confined to the bedroom for a full three months. One day he had taken to his bed, following an attack, no doubt, and when he had left it, he had, as the concierge put it, weighed no more than a child of ten.

Etienne almost cried out, in panic. He got up and roamed around the apartment in search of Fernande. He found her in the spare room. She was surprised to see him, wondering what he wanted.

He had nothing to say to her. It was just that he longed for the sight of a human being, someone fit and active, bustling around the place.

"Can I do anything for you?"

He tried to think of something, but could not.

"No."

Louise must have heard him moving. When he got back to the bedroom, she was coming up the stairs.

"What are you doing?"

"Nothing."

"Are you bored?"

Perhaps she was sorry for him, as one is sorry for a cat when one has no choice but to drown it.

He could not bring himself to bear her any ill will. He felt that she was not to blame.

Was he not as guilty as she was? Had he not always shrunk from questioning her?

He had kept silent, and so had she—for fifteen years. And, because they had to have something to hold on to, because, in their insecurity, they always had to be proving to themselves that they had each other, they had made love desperately.

He had always known the truth, even while he had refused to face it. That was why he needed her so.

"Would you like me to stay with you for a bit?"

He shook his head.

"Where are you going to sit?"

"I don't know."

He thought he was going to faint. He fought against it with all his strength. He wanted to take hold of her by the shoulders, to draw her to him until her face was close to his, to look into her eyes, as he did when she lay in his arms, and to cry out to her:

"Once and for all you've got to listen to me: you killed Guillaume because you wanted me, and I've always known it. I suspected it the very first day. I didn't stop you. I let you do it. I didn't say a word. Because I loved you. Because I wanted you, too. Because there had never been any other woman in my life.

"I married you.

"I've lived with you in this house for fifteen years. We've done everything that a man and a woman can do to become one flesh. We've been the taste in each other's mouths, the sweat of each other's bodies.

"You and I are caught in a trap together, and our bed has become our universe.

"Look at me, Louise.

"A hundred times, you've implored me never to leave you.

"Now it's my turn to die, and it's you who are killing me. I know. I can feel it. I've taken Guillaume's place in this room. Because there's someone downstairs, perhaps, or on Rue Lepic, who has taken the place I once had.

"Tell me the truth. Admit it.

"Tell me his name!"

"What's the matter with you?" she asked.

He was vaguely aware of opening his eyes, and seeing her

there, looking anxiously at him. His lips shaped the final words of his unspoken appeal:

"*Have pity on me!*"

He drew his hand across his forehead. It was covered in sweat. He swayed.

She hurriedly pushed a chair toward him.

"Sit down," she said.

She helped him into the chair. He was trembling violently.

"What is it you feel? Do you want me to send for the doctor?"

He shook his head.

"A glass of water?"

"No."

"You shouldn't have got up."

"Louise!"

"Yes?"

He swallowed, struggling to pull himself together. He wanted his voice to sound calm and detached.

"Do you still love me?"

He already knew. She had given a little start, which had not escaped him. Now, too late, she was trying to smile:

"What a ridiculous question!"

"That's no answer."

"Well, then, yes, of course."

Her expression, he felt, was not without warmth, even affection, but he now knew with absolute certainty that she no longer loved him.

"You can go down now," he whispered.

"I'm staying with you."

He gave a slight shrug. What was the good of arguing? It made no difference now whether she stayed or went.

"As soon as you get your breath back, I'll put you to bed."

"No."

Suddenly the bed, even the room, seemed menacing.

"What do you want to do?"

"Nothing."

What could he do? Guillaume, too, must have asked her in anguish whether she loved him still, and she, impatient to get away to the room on Rue Lepic, must have replied, in the very same way:

"What a ridiculous question!"

Unless, perhaps, Guillaume had not noticed anything wrong. There had been no precedent then. *He* had not been her accomplice.

"Are you cold?"

"No."

"Your hands are frozen."

He waved her away. It was so sudden that he could not get to the bathroom, or even as far as the edge of the carpet. He had barely the strength to get up from his chair and lean forward before he vomited his coffee, in a stream that spread over the floor to the middle of the dining room.

"I'm sorry," he stammered, both hands clasped to his chest.

Mechanically she replied:

"It's not your fault."

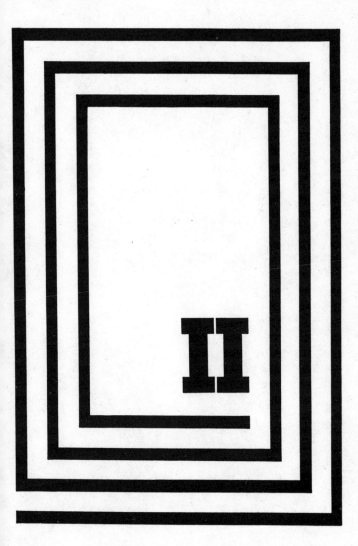

It was a Tuesday, the second since he had made up his mind that he would neither die nor give up Louise. After lunch, he had made two calls on customers who he knew would not detain him, and, since half past two, he had been sitting, at a table by the window, in a café on Avenue des Ternes.

Across the avenue, sandwiched between a shoe store and a large grocery store with goods displayed on trestles on the sidewalk, was an apartment house. On the left-hand side of the door, when there was a gap in the stream of traffic, he could see a cheap enamel plate, and though at that distance he could not decipher the inscription, he knew that it read "*Albert Doër, Doctor of Medicine,*" and that the doctor's office hours were engraved in smaller lettering underneath. He had ordered a small bottle of Vichy water, but was not drinking it, for fear that the mineral salts would spoil the tests. As almost invariably happened on Tuesdays, he had eaten lamb cutlets and mashed potatoes, and now, sitting on the café bench with his sample case beside him, he was waiting for the attack to begin.

For the first time, he was hoping for it, and, staring fixedly at nothing, he concentrated all his attention on the functioning of his body, pressing his finger to his left wrist once in a while, to check his pulse.

Apart from himself, there was no one in the café but a fat countrywoman surrounded by parcels. Her eyes were red with weeping, and the way she kept looking first at the clock, then at the door, with an expression of acute anxiety, had begun to irritate him.

He was in no mood to waste sympathy on other people, and she was just the kind of woman to start up a conversation and pour out all her woes. Now and then, her lips moved as though she were praying. Once or twice their glances met, but each time he looked away, conscious that she was only waiting for a chance to speak to him. She was dressed in black, wearing a new dress under her coat, and a new hat. She must be in mourning. Perhaps she had come to Paris to at end a funeral? He thought it more likely that she had been recently widowed and had made the journey to see her daughte , who was probably in service with some respectable family.

The girl had not turned up. Very likely, she wou d not come at all.

To kill time, the mother had already eaten three or four brioches. Maybe she would never see her daughter again.

Screened from the café by a partition about the height of a man was a bar, with people resting their elbows on the counter. They could be heard talking, and spitting on the floor. From time to time, the waiter came in to see whether he and the fat woman were still there, and to ask if they needed anything.

He had made a point of eating more than usual at lunch. Afterward, there was nothing to do but wait, and he had called on the two customers, small tradespeople whose billing forms were printed by Monsieur Théo, simply to pass the time. He had not drunk any coffee. The peasant woman who was trying to attract his attention, in the delusion that her problems were of great interest, was far from suspecting the nature of his own preoccupations. All she could see was a well-dressed, respectable gentleman with a case of samples, and a glass of mineral water in front of him.

Once, she sighed so deeply that he found himself looking straight at her, but, by turning quickly toward the door, he just managed to prevent her speaking to him.

The previous Tuesday's visit had produced no conclusive results. It just happened to be a Tuesday, in the morning, and he had eaten only his breakfast of coffee and croissants. For some days before that, he had eaten virtually nothing.

It had been rather embarrassing at first. He had waited over an hour, and when, at last, he went into the consulting room, he saw that, although the doctor knew his face, he could not quite recall the object of his first visit, and was searching his memory for a clue. Etienne reckoned that he must see forty or more patients a day, most of them strangers, whom he would never set eyes on again.

"I came to see you once before, about my heart."

The doctor nodded.

"Undress, please."

"That isn't what I've come about today. There are one or two questions I should like to ask you."

The doctor's waiting room was full of people. He had to work on the conveyor-belt system. Etienne's preamble worried him. Automatically, he glanced toward the door.

"Suppose a man had been having a certain amount of arsenic regularly over a period. . . ."

The doctor's expression changed. Etienne had been prepared for this, but had made up his mind to go through with it.

"I was wondering if there was any way of confirming it scientifically."

The lower half of the window was of frosted glass. Beside it was a folding table used for examining patients. It was covered with oilcloth and spread with a towel that was none too clean. Laid out on an enamel trolley were forceps, specula, and other surgical instruments. Etienne did not know what they were for, and tried to avoid looking at them.

"Do you know what I mean?"

There had been entreaty in his eyes then, and his voice had faltered. He had felt, that morning, that his fate was in the balance.

"In effect, what you're asking me is whether someone who thinks he is being poisoned can have medical tests to prove it?"

Etienne nodded, but did not lower his eyes. Now it was the doctor who showed signs of embarrassment, and his glance rested for a second or two on the wedding ring on Etienne's left hand.

"It is, of course, possible, provided the dose is large enough."

"How is it done?"

"First, a urine test—that's the most reliable. Then, a blood test. I say provided the dose is large enough, because one finds traces of arsenious oxide in most organisms."

"Could you do the tests?"

The doctor hesitated, looked searchingly at him, and then asked in an undertone:

"Do you live in this district?"

He lied:

"Porte Péreire."

"Have you serious grounds for believing that you have been taking arsenic without knowing it?"

"I think it's possible."

Did the doctor take him for a lunatic or a neurotic? With obvious reluctance, he handed him a glass receptacle and said:

"Pass water, please."

Meanwhile, keeping Etienne under observation the whole time, summing him up, the doctor was sterilizing the syringe and needle for the blood test.

"Take off your jacket, and roll up your left shirt sleeve."

Etienne, who could not endure the sight of his own blood, kept his eyes fixed on the window. It seemed to him that in this place his skin looked even more blanched than it did on Boulevard de Clichy.

"How long, in your opinion, might you have been having arsenic?"

"I don't know exactly. Several weeks, possibly several months."

"Have you lost a lot of weight?"

"Yes."

"Have you ever had abdominal pains, with a burning sensation in the throat?"

"Yes."

"Do you suffer from palpitations?"

"That was why I came to see you in the first place."

He knew that he had given all the right answers, because he had looked up the effects of arsenic in an encyclopedia. The doctor seemed worried.

"I can't do the tests now. It's quite a long job. Come and

see me tomorrow morning. If you can't manage it, call me and I'll let you know the result."

It was obvious that he was anxious to be paid there and then.

"How much do I owe you?"

He hesitated for a moment, then said:

"Five thousand francs."

Etienne had thought it advisable to come himself the next day, and when the doctor caught sight of him at the back of the line, he attended to him before the other patients. Was this significant? Etienne already had the look of a condemned man.

"When we were discussing your problem yesterday, I overlooked the delicacy of the situation. It's putting a heavy responsibility on me to ask for the results of tests of this nature, and I have some misgivings as to whether, in giving you such information, I might not be guilty of unprofessional conduct."

"Surely, as it concerns my state of health, and you are a doctor . . . ?"

"There may be others involved besides yourself. If you had taken arsenic by accident, it would be a different matter. I must emphasize that my diagnosis is by no means conclusive. Do I make myself clear?"

He was emphatic, serious, troubled, as though he were discussing an abortion, or some other illegal operation.

"The fact is that I did find traces of arsenious oxide, not in the urine, but in the blood, which suggests that the poison was not administered very recently. On the other hand, the amount is not large enough to indicate positively that someone is trying to poison you."

For no apparent reason, Etienne had had an attack the

previous afternoon. Was it because he had been upset by his interview with the doctor that morning?

"Is there no way of finding out for certain?"

"It would be necessary to take samples fairly soon after the poison has been taken, and before the system begins to eliminate it."

"Would you mind if I came back next Tuesday?"

"That's up to you."

The doctor had not asked him why Tuesday, rather than any other day, but he must have understood what was in Etienne's mind, because he had looked at him more searchingly than on the previous day, and it was obvious that he was acutely embarrassed.

"If you do come, I'll try to fit you in at once," he said, glancing at the sample case.

As he was seeing Etienne to the door, the doctor asked, in a more casual tone:

"Are you a businessman?"

He had said that he was, but the doctor knew enough about people to guess that he was a commercial traveler.

It would be just his luck if there were no attack today, and he cheated a little by leaning forward so that the edge of the table pressed on his stomach. He had discovered some time ago that he could induce at will a sensation akin to heart spasms. First, there would be a rather sharp, localized pain, not always in the same spot, but invariably on the left side; this would then spread in waves to his shoulder, and sometimes to the crook of his elbow.

For instance, he had only to think of things that he preferred to forget, in particular of the last weeks of Guillaume Gatin's life, in the room linked by the iron staircase to the shop below.

During those three days in bed, after vomiting on the dining-room carpet, he had merged his identity with that of Louise's first husband, and had even felt a measure of relief in sinking deeper and deeper into an abyss, the horrors of which God alone knew.

He had neither washed nor shaved, wallowing in his filth, and had refused to allow his wife to sponge his body or even his face.

He had lost the will to live. He saw his life ebbing slowly away, and made no effort to fight back. He had refused to look anyone in the face, whether it was his wife or Fernande or Dr. Maresco, whom Louise had called in, and whose examination he had endured in complete silence.

He did not want to dwell on the thoughts that had obsessed him during those three days, the most loathsome of his whole life. Besides, it would not have been true to say that he had wantonly resigned himself to death, since he had refused all food other than bread and butter, which he believed it would be difficult to poison.

He had drunk nothing but water, never taking his eyes off Louise or Fernande while she filled his glass from the bathroom tap. Sometimes he even sniffed surreptitiously at the hand that held out the glass to him.

Pretending that strong light was a strain on his eyes, he had the green velvet curtains drawn over both windows, so that he lay the whole day with the bedside lamp switched on, and only a narrow crack between the curtains to distinguish night from day. He had thought a great deal about his childhood, his mother, and his father, whom he resembled physically, and he had wondered for the first time whether his father had been a happy man.

His mother was still living in Lyons, in a little suburban

house that she had bought after her husband's death, though Etienne could not imagine how she had managed it. She had always complained of being short of money, and during his early years in Paris, Etienne had sent her half his earnings.

Louise had run up and down the stairs twenty times a day, without a word of complaint. Once, he had tried to picture her as a nurse, in a white uniform and starched cap. She would have made a good nurse.

From time to time, without realizing it, he had returned to the surface of life, and his thoughts had grown less somber, but, the moment he became aware of this, he sank back into the abyss.

One night, with Louise lying so close to him that he could feel the warmth of her body, he had composed a confession, complete in every detail and every word, such as he might make to a priest. Not just to any priest, but to the parish priest with the ascetic cast of face whom he had known as a child, and who had heard his first confession.

It had seemed to him that he could hear the murmur of questions through the grille of the confessional. He revealed everything, including things he had never before been willing to face as they really were, things buried for years in the twilight of his unconscious mind.

Nothing had been lost, he had forgotten nothing. Everything had come back to him with cruel distinctness.

Never had he thought of Louise so passionately and yet so clear-sightedly. Never had he so well understood his relationship with her.

Had he not, from the very first day, been a little afraid of her?

Why had he refused to admit it to himself? It was the truth. After leaving the shop that, only a little time before, he had regarded as just another stationer's, he had known that here was a threat to everything he had been, everything he had known till then, a threat to his whole way of life.

Boarding the bus, he had been so well aware of this that he had asked himself whether there was not still time to escape.

The most difficult thing to put into words had been the precise impression that she had made on him. Had he perhaps been aware, from the first, that she was stronger than he, that, in her, life blazed like an unquenchable fire?

It was because of this fire, this passion that burned into him from her eyes and her lips, and breathed life into every particle of his flesh, that he had loved her abjectly, and later realized that he could never give her up.

He had included all this, and much more that was true, in his confession, until at last his grief could find no outlet but in tears.

Louise's hand had touched his thigh, and she had whispered:

"Are you asleep?"

"No."

"Are you crying?"

He had replied:

"It's my cold."

There had been another bed, before this one, in the same room, in the same place, with a man lying in it beside Louise, and, when they had taken him away, he had weighed no more than a child of ten.

Thus, for three days and three nights, he had wrestled with phantoms, and when, from time to time, they left him in peace, he would deliberately conjure them up again. Then, on the afternoon of the fourth day, after having lain for a long time staring at the bedside lamp, he had got up and gone to the window to draw back the curtains.

The boulevard was bathed in sunshine. All trace of the fair had gone, and the passers-by were crunching dead leaves underfoot.

His only fear, now that he had come to a decision, had been that Louise might come up the stairs before he had time to finish what he had to do, but he had so managed things that she had not heard a sound.

As soon as he was ready, he had gone to the head of the iron staircase, and had called down in a strong voice, in which there was no hint of the terrors he had endured:

"Louise!"

Realizing that the voice had not come from the bed, she had rushed toward the stairs, puzzled and anxious. Halfway up, she had caught sight of him, and had stood staring in stupefaction.

She had been so staggered to find him dressed, freshly shaved, with a little smile on his lips, that he almost felt sorry for her.

"Are you up?"

Why, at that moment, had he thought of his mother? She had had the same way of looking at him whenever he had shown kindness or affection, as though she believed that he was only doing it to put her in a good humor, that there must be a catch to it.

When he reproached her for mistrusting him, she would say with a sigh:

"I know you so well!"

Louise dared not show her mistrust.

"Are you feeling better?"

"I've got something to say to you. It can't wait until this evening. Come with me."

He opened the dining-room door, because he felt that he could talk more easily in there than in the bedroom, which still reeked of his illness.

"Have you been very worried?" he asked. His face wore a gentle expression.

"Yes . . . of course . . ."

"I called you because I want to ask you to forgive me for all the trouble I've given you. Oh yes, I have! I know what I'm talking about. I don't quite know what came over me. A kind of nervous breakdown, I think."

He did not believe it. He had rehearsed his little speech while lying in bed, almost reciting it out loud to get the right intonation.

Since he wanted to go on living, this was the only way. Either it must be done this way, or he must leave her. He did not want that. He was not going to lose Louise. He had made up his mind to keep her in spite of herself.

Suddenly he felt strong, almost as strong as Louise, and the strangest thing was that he found himself living his part, feeling genuinely moved, looking at her with real tenderness.

"Are you very angry with me?"

"Why should I be?"

He just stopped himself from saying:

"Because I doubted your good faith."

Just in time, he saw the dangers of such an admission. She would guess what he had suspected.

This must be avoided at all costs. He must, on the contrary, set her mind at rest; otherwise she might be tempted to speed things up by giving him a stronger dose.

"You know, I think it must be my stomach. One always hears that stomach troubles make people irritable, and I'm beginning to think it's true. Let's face it, I've been impossible."

At last, she smiled, a mere ghost of a smile, and said:

"I must say, you really did frighten me. I was at my wits' end. It didn't help for Dr. Maresco to tell me over and over again that there was nothing seriously wrong with you."

Everything was shining, the highly polished furniture, the plates on the dresser, the silver dishes on the sideboard.

He made a tentative gesture, as though unsure of himself, and she came toward him. He put his arm about her waist and felt her rounded breasts against his chest.

"Will you forgive me?" he whispered in her ear.

"Idiot!" she whispered back, and then pressed her mouth against his.

When, that night, he had wanted to make love to her, she had tried halfheartedly to dissuade him:

"Won't it tire you?"

He was determined that everything be as before, that nothing be changed. He had already made up his mind to see the doctor on Avenue des Ternes next morning. His plan was worked out to the last detail.

Since then, everything had gone as he intended, though he was not certain that she was entirely reassured. She was still watching him, and he was on the alert for her every look and gesture.

On Thursday evening, Mariette, too, had started at seeing him.

"You frightened us!" she said teasingly. "You can't imagine how terribly upset Louise has been."

No doubt this remark had irked Louise. Mariette was overdoing it. She never knew when to keep her mouth shut.

Arthur Leduc, perhaps, was more perceptive. All evening he had seemed ill at ease, as though he sensed something disquieting in the atmosphere of the house.

One day, should it become necessary, Etienne would speak to him. He could always run him to earth in one of the Montmartre cafés where he played *belote,* and it would be their first meeting, man to man, on neutral ground.

His feeling was that he would be able to tell immediately whether or not he could count on Arthur's support. If his first impression was favorable, then he would tell him everything. There was just one obstacle, as far as he could see. He suspected that Louise had helped Arthur and Mariette financially when they were in difficulties, and Leduc was not the man to repay kindness with disloyalty. He would have to go very cautiously.

On Sunday, as it had been too cold to walk around the streets, they had gone to the Médrano Circus, and then dined at the Brasserie Lorraine.

Physically, Etienne was not fully recovered. He still felt very weak, but said nothing about it, and called on the customers as usual. It was a relief to be out of the house, not having to watch his step the whole time. Often, a bitter and ironic smile came to his lips at the thought of his predicament, and the part he was playing.

This thought would strike him in the middle of the street, with people milling around him, all wrapped up in their own petty affairs. Whoever could have had an inkling, seeing him walking along with his case in his hand, of the drama that he was living through?

What must be avoided at all costs was for Louise to lose her head and finish him off before he could forestall her. This course, however, would not be without risk to her, for if she acted prematurely, the doctors might suspect the truth.

Had Dr. Rivet had any suspicions, that other time?

He was not wholly convinced that he had not. The old doctor had always looked at him in a peculiar way, with an air at once contemptuous and ironic.

No doubt, like a good many other people, the doctor had believed that he had married Louise for her money.

Maresco was the kind to sign his death certificate without question, whether or not the cause of death was apparent.

The thought of death was less frightening to him now that he had decided not to die. For now it was up to him and no one else. His will and his nerve would determine the issue.

He must discover Louise's secret as quickly as possible. He had already completed the important, preliminary task of sifting the evidence and discarding unlikely theories.

Toward the end of the three days, as he had lain in bed thinking the whole thing out, he had almost made up his mind never to leave the house again, and, by remaining an invalid, to keep the closest possible watch on his wife.

However, he had very soon realized that this was a clumsy and dangerous plan, and had thought better of it. He had also given up all idea of searching the apartment for poison. Once, sweating and in his bare feet, he had rummaged through his wife's bureau, and then gone back to bed discouraged.

If Louise had slipped out of the building during the past week, it could only have been for a very short time. He had made sure of this by speaking to her on the telephone at frequent but irregular intervals, giving as his excuse that he wanted to say hello, and find out how she was.

Occasionally, too, especially at the times when she used to

come to him on Rue Lepic in the old days, he waited, out of sight, on the corner of Place Blanche, keeping the house under observation, making a mental note of all the people who went into the shop, and of how long they stayed.

On Saturday morning at about ten, he was keeping watch in this way when the concierge went past, very close to him. He could not tell whether or not she had seen him, but, even if she had, she would be unlikely to mention it to Louise, whom she liked scarcely better than she liked him.

The peasant woman in mourning was fidgeting on the bench, and the hands of the clock pointed to several minutes past three. If Louise had any inkling of his suspicions, she would stop the doses of poison for a while.

Barely ten days ago, he had thought of these things only in vague terms, with the same shamefaced apprehension that thoughts of sex had aroused in him as a child.

Now, he was looking facts in the face, and he was proud of it. The word "poison" was inscribed on his brain in bold red letters, like those on the bottles at the pharmacy.

He was beginning to feel sick. His hopes rose, but just at that moment the peasant woman banged her spoon on the saucer to attract the waiter's attention. Etienne could not help overhearing what she was saying:

"I wonder if you happen to know a little fair girl, a bit plump, with curly hair? Her name is Elise, and she works around here."

"What does she do?" the waiter asked politely, winking at Etienne.

"She's in service."

"Did she say she'd meet you here? Are you sure you've come to the right place?"

She took a crumpled letter from her handbag, and showed it to him, underlining the relevant words with her finger.

"Yes, this is the place," he agreed. "Don't you know her employers' name?"

"All I know is that they're in business, and that they have two children."

Etienne stood up abruptly. He had already paid, but he had to go back to fetch his case, which he had left lying on the bench. Because of this woman, he was unsure of himself. If this was the beginning of an attack, it was not a severe one. All the same, his throat was dry and burning, and he felt a dull pain in his head.

He crossed the avenue, and went upstairs to the doctor's office. He was delighted to see that there were only three patients in the waiting room, which was usually full of people. He waited ten minutes or so, hearing voices in the inner room, then the scraping of the folding table and, at last, approaching footsteps.

"Thank you, doctor."

"Come back next Saturday at the same time."

It was a young woman. She looked exhausted, as though she had just undergone painful treatment, and he remembered the rows of instruments on the trolley.

Doër had seen him. Etienne waited for him to speak.

"You have an appointment, haven't you?"

This was for the benefit of the other patients, who might resent being kept waiting on his account.

The door closed. Etienne removed his overcoat, put his case down on a chair, and took the glass receptacle that the doctor held out to him.

"Do you feel anything?"

119

"I think so."

"When did it start?"

"About half an hour ago."

With his watch in his hand, the doctor took his pulse. He seemed more flustered than last time.

"Look straight in front of you."

With a little electric lamp strapped to his forehead, the doctor examined his eyes. It was painful when he turned back the lids.

"What do you feel?"

"Just the same as the other times, only less acute."

"When did you eat last?"

"We had lunch at half past twelve."

"Could you make yourself vomit?"

"Easily."

He had only to push his finger down his throat, and he vomited into an enamel bowl, then mopped his face and wiped his eyes.

"Aren't you going to do a blood test?"

"It may not be necessary."

The doctor looked at the time.

"Can you spare a moment?"

The thought that he would not have to wait until the next day for the result threw him into a fever of excitement.

"Sit down. It will only take a few minutes."

He took the two receptacles into a laboratory that was scarcely larger than a cupboard. He left the door ajar, but Etienne could not bring himself to watch him as he worked. He was suddenly terrified. His knees were trembling. He felt safer sitting where he was.

He heard the gas being turned on, then the hiss of the blue flame and the clinking of glass. He could not help remembering that, the week before, the doctor had charged him five thousand francs, on the grounds that it was a long job. Doër must have forgotten.

"Have you taken any kind of medicine in the last few days?"

"None at all."

He thought back for a moment, then corrected himself. He wanted to be absolutely accurate.

"Yes. The night before last, I took two aspirin."

It took longer than he had expected. The patients in the waiting room must be growing restive. It was a full twenty minutes before the doctor came out of his cubbyhole, and stood for a moment, dazzled by the light. There was a wash-basin in the room, behind a screen. He went to it, washed his hands, and slowly dried them, without saying a word or looking at Etienne.

"Naturally, I haven't had time to work out the exact dose, but you probably aren't so much concerned about that?"

"You found something?"

He nodded.

"More than you would normally expect?"

"No doubt about it."

"Enough to . . ."

He thought he was going to faint. Although it was what he had expected, he felt lightheaded. His heart seemed suddenly drained of blood, and there was a pounding in his ears.

He could not bring himself to say the word.

"Without the slightest doubt, enough to make anybody sick."

The doctor was ill at ease. From the first, Etienne had been sure that there was something shady about his practice, and, judging from the number of young women he had noticed in the waiting room, he guessed that it might be abortions.

Doër was pacing the room, troubled, watching his patient out of the corner of his eye.

At last, he came to a standstill, towering over Etienne.

"What are you going to do?" he asked.

Etienne could not find anything to say. He was unprepared for that particular question. He could not see where it was leading, until the doctor went on:

"Are you thinking of going to the police?"

Such a course had never occurred to him, and it must have shown in his expression.

"No."

"Why not?"

"I don't know. I . . ."

He would have had to tell Doër the whole story, to discuss Louise with him, and Etienne simply could not do it. What he needed to know was how much longer he could expect to live, if the poisoning were to continue at the present rate.

"You're putting me in a very delicate position," the doctor said in a low voice, running his hand over his bald head. "Ordinarily, I would have to report this to the police."

"But . . ."

Etienne was trembling violently, panic-stricken at the thought that the doctor might ruin his whole plan.

"You can't do it!" he almost screamed, springing to his feet.

"Please listen to me. You came here, asking me to test your urine and so on for arsenic. . . ."

"That's quite right."

"Well, I've found arsenic—quite a large amount. But what I don't know is whether you took it accidentally, or with something else in mind. Do you understand me?"

"Yes."

"All the same, for my own peace of mind, I would be glad to know your intentions, at least as far as any other person's involvement is concerned. Have you anyone in mind?"

He did not reply.

"It looks as though it must be a member of your household. What do you mean to do?"

"Nothing," he said quickly, both to set the doctor's mind at rest, and because it was quite close to the truth.

The very idea that Doër might pick up the telephone, call the police, and tell them the whole story, filled him with terror. Once he was out of the office, lost among the crowds on the avenue, he would feel safe again.

He had not given his name. The doctor did not know where he lived. Any description he might give of him should be fairly vague, and unlikely to be of much use in tracing him. Just at that moment, he caught sight of his initials on his sample case, and surreptitiously turned it around.

"I give you my word," he said very softly, "that I won't make any trouble for you."

He was carrying more money than usual. Not daring to ask his wife for such a large sum, he had managed, in anticipation of his visit to the doctor, to raise it that morning without telling her. On some trumped-up pretext, he had collected a cash payment from a customer. He would have to make it up somehow, before the end of the month.

That would come later. What mattered now, this minute, was to get out of this place.

"I swear to you, I don't mean to do anything wrong."

Why did the doctor seem so nonplused? Was there anything so very strange in what he had said?

It was not clear to him until later, when he was out in the

street, and a fair distance from Avenue des Ternes, where he was determined never to set foot again. He could not take the risk of bumping into Doër.

He had pulled his wallet out of his pocket and held out the ten thousand-franc notes contained in it, with too obvious eagerness.

Maybe the doctor needed the money because he, too, was living through some private drama? He stared at the notes, reddened, and then, at last, took them.

"The best of luck to you," he said.

He was letting him go against his better judgment, and he was not proud of the fact.

"I hope I'll see you again," he said, opening the door. Etienne stumbled blindly out of the room and down the stairs.

He felt no physical discomfort. He had not had a genuine attack that day. On the avenue, he threaded his way through the thick of the crowd, and, on Place des Ternes, he ran down the steps of the subway station.

He was still unsure of himself. The car was almost empty. He had no idea where he was going. When he saw the words "Place Clichy" he got out onto the platform, and walked slowly to the exit.

Now that he knew, now that he was sure, he would have to sort things out in his mind, and, above all, more than ever, avoid arousing Louise's suspicions.

Had Guillaume known, too?

It was better not to think of it. Thinking of it was dangerous, since he had decided that he was going to stay alive.

All the same, when he got as far as the bus terminal, he felt the need to go into a bistro and order a drink. As he drank it, he stared searchingly at himself reflected in the mirror, between two bottles.

Three days later, on Friday, he returned to Boulevard de Clichy as usual at about a quarter past six. The shutters were down over the shop front, and, before going under the archway, he glanced, as he always did, at the lighted mezzanine windows.

He had his key, though frequently, before he had time to fit it into the lock, Louise, recognizing his step on the stairs, would open the door for him. This evening, she did not do so. She was not in the bedroom. The dining-room door was open, but she was not in there, either. He was just going into the bathroom, where he supposed she must be washing her hands, when he saw her coming out of the kitchen, wearing a checkered apron over her dark dress. She was carrying a pile of plates, which she took to the dining-room table, on which the cloth was already spread.

"Isn't Fernande here?" he asked in astonishment.

"She walked out on me this afternoon."

She spoke quite naturally, but, although she studiously avoided looking at him, he suspected that she was on the alert for his reactions. She set out the plates, and went to fetch the silver from the drawer.

"I just happened to call her on the speaking tube at about three o'clock, otherwise I wouldn't have known she was gone until after we'd closed. When I didn't get any answer, I went upstairs and found the place empty. The dirty dishes from lunch were still in the sink."

It could be true. Maids—from cowardice, perhaps, or to flaunt their independence—had a way of leaving their employers without a word of warning. He was no longer sure of anything, but he gave no sign of it, outwardly behaving as naturally as she did.

What of her? Did she know that he was playing a part?

"I went up to the sixth floor, and found her bedroom door wide open. I could see she'd taken all her things. The bed wasn't made, and she'd left everything in a filthy state. It was revolting."

She went to the kitchen to lower the gas under a saucepan, and came back with bread and butter.

"While I was up there, I heard someone creeping around in the corridor, and then old Madame Coin appeared."

She, too, had lived in the building much longer than he had. She was a widow, living alone in one of the attic rooms on the sixth floor, the only one not occupied by a servant. In the past, she had done sewing for the people of the neighborhood, but now she was too old, and partially crippled.

She could be seen in the street any morning, carrying an ancient basket, and wearing a most peculiar hat. In all weather, summer and winter alike, she went out in her slippers, because she could no longer squeeze her swollen feet into shoes, and she shuffled along so slowly that the policeman had to stop the traffic for her to cross the road.

Louise went on:

" *'Good riddance!'* she said. *'You did right to throw her out —such scum!'*

"I asked her whether she knew what time it was when Fernande left.

"She said:

" *'Quite some time ago. One of her boy friends was there helping her take her things downstairs, and they took their time over it, fooling around without even bothering to shut the door. I hope the next one is a bit less noisy. That one was up to no good—a different man in with her every night—the kind I'd be frightened to meet on the stairs.'* "

Neither he nor Louise had known about this night life of Fernande's. They had not even suspected it. He remembered watching her make his bed while he had the flu, and wondering what she made of them, of him, but otherwise he had never given her a thought.

Louise took up the tale again.

"It seems," she said, "that quite often, when she came down in the morning, she left one of the boy friends in her room. Some of them were in there half the day, sleeping, and she used to take food up to them. I found an old razor lying around."

"Have you got someone else?"

"I called the agency. They're sending me a girl tomorrow morning. Dinner will be ready in a few minutes."

What his wife had said about Fernande was plausible, it rang true. His wife had certainly not invented old Madame Coin's part in the affair: it could be so easily checked. On the other hand, she had not necessarily told him the whole story. Was it possible that she had wanted Fernande out of the way?

Like his mother, who never took anything on trust, he was probing for a hidden meaning in everything that Louise did or said. That evening, he read the paper while she washed up, but she was never out of his thoughts.

The disturbing thing was that he did not know what she was thinking. In their fifteen years together, he had never needed to consider the question. Now, for the first time, he realized how very close to each other they had grown over the years.

The truth was that in spite of the tragedy that they were living through together, in the seclusion of their home, they could not bring themselves to think of each other as enemies.

If Louise felt as he did, then it took no effort for her to speak to him in the same tone, and look at him in the same way, as she had always done.

He was ashamed of the way he had spied on her and, in a sense, deceived her, in the last few weeks. But it had to be done. It was his only chance of survival.

It grieved him nonetheless. He was without rancor. He was ready to swear that there was no hatred in his heart. At times, indeed, he pitied her.

Her part was more difficult than his, more dangerous and more cruel, since she lived in constant fear of being found out.

On the night of the *belote* session with the Leducs, when she had made the mistake of shutting herself in the bedroom with Mariette, and Etienne had lost control of himself, she had been certain that he had guessed everything.

Since then he had done all he could to make her believe that she had been mistaken. Had he succeeded? Had he played his part convincingly?

He had no wish to make Louise suffer. He knew very well that her present state of uncertainty must be unbearable.

The previous night, Mariette and her husband had dined with them again. He had not noticed anything amiss. They had both congratulated him on looking so well. At *belote*, the Leducs had played as partners against them, which they had not done for a long time. He and Louise had won one of the two rubbers. They had backed each other up all the way through, while Arthur had reproached Mariette more than once for not responding to his bids.

When the dishes were done, Louise went into the bathroom to freshen up, then settled down in her chair to sew on his shirt buttons.

Etienne was not finding it easy to keep to his plan. He had to resort to so many tricks that he wondered how long he could go on without being found out.

For instance, when there was a dish that Louise did not eat —starchy food in particular, like the lima beans at lunch— he always took care to make himself vomit as soon as possible after the meal. He dared not do it at home, in case she should hear him. On the other hand, he was anxious to lose no time, as he had forgotten to ask Doër how long the poison took to act.

He had to gulp down his coffee, and, instead of lingering in the apartment as he had always done, grab his coat and his case and rush out into the street. Each time, he had to make some excuse for his haste. It was not easy. He did not have far to go, just to a small bar on the other side of Place Blanche, where he made straight for the toilet.

The proprietor obviously thought it very odd. He would have to avoid going too often to any one place. It would not do to make himself conspicuous. It was just as well that he never had anything but soup, cold meat, and cheese in the evening, as he could not have found a plausible reason for going out alone after dinner.

He had never done such a thing. They had been so much on their own, so cut off from the rest of the world, that the smallest deviation was an event in their lives.

Since he had made the first advances, Louise had gone back to undressing without switching on the light, in the shadowy glow from outside, which, now that the fair had gone, was permeated with the deep red of the neon sign. There was only one thing that she still dared not venture, to stretch out on the bed and call to him:

"Are you coming?"

He did not have to make an effort when she was in his arms, far from it. She was not pretending, either, and sometimes, when it struck him that she might be thinking of the other man, he worked himself up into such a frenzy that it must have seemed as though, in his despair, he was bent on destroying her. Once, at least, he had seen fear in her eyes.

Since then, he had restrained himself. It was a strange, complicated existence, yet it gave him a kind of thrill.

The new maid arrived at eight o'clock next morning. Louise was already up and dressed, and had given him his breakfast. He was still dressing. He could hear their voices in the kitchen, and it sounded as though the girl were talking in a foreign language.

A few minutes later, Louise came in, looking worried.

"She's from Alsace. Do you mind?"

"Why should I?"

"Well, she can hardly speak a word of French. I think she understood me when I told her what to do, and she seems clean. She's come straight from her village. She has excellent references, including a letter from the mayor, singing her praises."

He had almost finished shaving, and his reflection in the mirror showed the beginning of a smile. He suppressed it quickly. He must not, on any account, let her catch him smiling in that way, for he sensed that things were coming to a head.

"What's bothering you?" he asked with studied casualness.

"I thought you might not like having someone around the house who can't speak our language."

He knew what was coming, and waited.

"To begin with, till she's used to things, I'll have to do the shopping myself."

It was almost more than he could do to keep a straight face.

"I don't think she'll take long to learn," Louise went on, watching him in the mirror.

And, with an air of complete indifference, he said:

"As long as she's clean and hard-working!"

"Shall I engage her, then?"

"Suit yourself. It's entirely up to you."

She lingered uncertainly for a few moments in the bathroom, before going out to speak to the Alsatian girl. A little later he saw the girl for himself. She was plump, with a clear skin and wholesome pink cheeks. Her manner was awkward, but she seemed very willing.

"I'm going down to let Monsieur Charles in, then I'll come back and show her the ropes. Have you a lot of calls today?"

"The Trinité round."

In this field, too, deceit was tricky and dangerous. Louise knew the customers as well as he did. Right from the start, she had always wanted to know where he was going, and she would sometimes leave a telephone message for him somewhere on his round, when, for instance, a customer wanted urgently to see him.

He had only recently become aware that, even out of the house, he was still tied to her apron strings.

He had somehow to make up the time he spent spying on Louise. This meant that he could no longer walk between calls, but instead had to cover much of the ground in taxis, a thing he had never done before.

Money was a problem, too. Dr. Doër had been expensive. Luckily, it was still only the eleventh, and he had until the thirty-first of the month to make up the amount that he had got from a customer without telling Louise.

As for eating, on the days when he had to vomit after his midday meal, he made do with a couple of hard-boiled eggs at a snack bar.

"Don't overdo it," she urged him that morning, as he kissed her before setting out.

Very likely, she meant nothing by it. All the same, it worried him. It was a Saturday, the sky was bright, and the air crisp. From time to time, a cloud drifted slowly across the sun, blotting it out for an instant; then the buildings were bathed in light once more.

He was seething with excitement. As he had no idea when his wife would be coming out to do the shopping, he had to stay close at hand, but he dared not stand very long in one spot, for fear of drawing attention to himself.

He crossed to the trees on the other side of the boulevard. He stood facing the Moulin-Rouge, taking care to keep out of sight behind the newspaper kiosk. Standing around, he was very conscious of the weight and bulk of his sample case. As long as he had it with him, he could scarcely hope to pass for a casual loafer. He was very much tempted to deposit it in a nearby café, but dared not risk it.

In the old days, when Louise had come to Rue Lepic, she had almost always set out at once after letting Monsieur Charles in; she could not get to him soon enough.

He saw the stockman leaving the subway station, then Monsieur Théo coming around the corner. In his black overcoat the printer looked older and more careworn than he did in his gray working overall.

Monsieur Charles raised the shutters. A few minutes later, the postman went through the archway, and then reappeared. Immediately afterward, the concierge came running after him, and handed him a letter that must have been delivered in error. She did not see Etienne. He was quite a long way from the house, and keeping well out of sight.

Sitting on one of the benches, watching Etienne, his eyes sparkling with malice, was an old man. He looked like a tramp. Etienne was irked by his presence. Ostentatiously, he paced up and down and looked at his watch, as though he were waiting for someone.

It was twenty-five minutes past nine—he had no need for his watch, there was an electric clock just across the road—when Louise came out of the shop, carrying a black plastic shopping bag. Looking to neither right nor left, she made for Rue Lepic. She walked along the street slowly, examining the fruit and vegetables piled on the rows of little barrows.

It was the first time that, unknown to her, he had seen her going about her daily life, passing by like a stranger, and it had an odd effect on him. She looked different, older perhaps, like Monsieur Théo. She was wearing last year's black woolen coat, and an old hat that he had forgotten.

There were a few others like her, among the housewives hurrying up and down the street: middle-aged, well-groomed, self-assured women in good clothes, whom the stall holders would accost with a coarse jest if they went past without stopping to buy. Until now, it had never occurred to him, when he had met such women, that they could still have love affairs.

He had pictured them in their gloomy but well-kept homes, with family photographs on the walls and mantelpieces. He had thought of them as comfortably off, with husbands in secure jobs, and children coming home from school in the evening. Only a short while ago, the idea that such women might have secret lives of their own would have seemed to him ridiculous and shocking. Indeed, he had assumed that at their age they had finished with love-making.

Shadowing Louise as she moved through the crowd was difficult and risky. If he kept too far behind her, he might lose sight of her, or—should she, for instance, go into a shop without his noticing—even find himself ahead of her. In that case, she would catch up with him, and he would be hard put to explain what he was doing there.

If he stayed too close to her and she turned around suddenly, he would bump right into her.

He moved forward as best he could, keeping his distance, lingering at the stalls. She bought leeks and a cabbage, then went into Deligeard's Dairy, where they were old customers. She was in the shop a long time, waiting to be served.

She was unaware of being followed. When she got to the top of the road, she turned right onto Rue des Abbesses, and he thought she was going to the butcher's, a few doors away. She went past the shop, however, and he had to hang back, because here the sidewalk was less crowded, and it was more difficult to keep out of sight.

Wherever she was heading for, it was not one of their regular shops. She was walking more briskly now, not like a woman buying her provisions at leisure, but purposefully, with a definite end in view, and when she reached Place des Abbesses, she dived into the post office.

She was not carrying any letters. It was Monsieur Charles's job to dispatch the mail, buy the stamps, and register the parcels.

He barely had time to take cover at the far end of a dimly lit bar, before she was out of the post office and coming back toward him. She was walking slowly now, almost dispiritedly.

The change struck him with greater force as he watched her go past on the other side of the road. A little while ago he had seen her for the first time as an aging woman. Now, she looked even older, a woman in her forty-seventh year, whose face, though not coarsened or wrinkled, had aged by slow degrees from within.

She was staring straight in front of her, looking pale and exhausted. She walked past the butcher's shop without seeing it, and had reached the end of the road before she realized it and turned back.

There was no point now in waiting. There was nothing more he could find out today, unless she were to come back in the afternoon. All the same, he continued to follow her, and it pained him to see her so distressed.

She went into the grocer's, and then, at last, turned onto Boulevard de Clichy and made for home. He jumped into a taxi and drove off toward the Trinité.

At lunchtime, she made an effort to behave normally, but

she was absent-minded, forgetful of the need to watch him, wrapped up in her own thoughts. He could see that she had been crying.

Watching her, it struck him that he had perhaps over-reached himself; the sudden improvement in his health was too obvious.

From then on he was always careful, when he got home, to hunch his shoulders and assume an air of weariness.

He made a number of calls. That evening, it was she who suggested going to the movies on Place Clichy. They stopped on the way back for a glass of beer. Possibly without thinking, because her mind was elsewhere, she switched on the bedroom light. It had come to be a signal. He made no protest, but got into bed and kissed her:

"Good night, Louise."

"Good night, Etienne."

She was on the verge of tears, but would hold them back until he fell asleep. It was he who repeated softly:

"Good night, Louise," in the old way.

She answered him. Much later, he whispered:

"Are you asleep?"

She was not asleep, he was sure, but she did not reply.

Sunday was overcast. The new girl, who was a Catholic, attended Mass, and then went up to the sixth floor to change out of her best clothes. Louise spent the rest of the morning, in her dressing gown, explaining the household routine to her, and showing her where everything was kept. They went through the apartment together with the vacuum cleaner.

Now that he was close to his goal, he was beginning to realize the gravity of his decision. He did not have to make much effort to appear a sick man; he was at all times obsessed with a single idea, uneasy and restless wherever he was.

They did not feel like going for a walk after lunch, yet now they both dreaded spending the afternoon alone together in the apartment. They went through the list of entertainments, considering two or three plays and a couple of films.

In the end, they walked toward the main boulevards, intending to go to a film that was having a very successful run.

There was a line over a hundred yards long outside the movie house, and they walked on. They found a place that was not full, but they had seen the film already.

There were other couples besides them lingering on the sidewalk, unable to make up their minds. It was growing late. Their legs were aching.

"What shall we do?"

They could not think of anything they wanted to do. They felt lost in the streets of Paris, in a crowd to which they did not belong.

Finally, they went into a dingy movie house near Porte Saint-Denis, after the show had started. They stayed to the end, for want of anything better to do, and, by the time they came out, it was night.

They had told the new maid, whose name was Emma, that they would not be in for dinner. They decided to go to a brasserie they knew, but by the time they got there it was crowded, and they had to wait for their seats.

"Isn't it a bore?" he said.

She replied, with a forced smile, that she did not mind. She was driven to lying, just as he was. They were both committed to a game of bluff, and neither could tell how far the other was taken in.

The day before, she had gone to the post office to collect a letter. She had been expecting it, maybe for several days, but it had not come. Next morning, she would go back to Place des Abbesses. Would there be anything for her this time?

When they got home, she seemed irresolute. He could see that she did not want to make love but was afraid of arousing his suspicions.

Since he felt as she did, he said that he was tired and had a stomach ache.

"Good night, Louise."

"Good night, Etienne."

In the drowsy state between waking and sleeping, he began to count the number of times they had said this to each other —three hundred and sixty-five multiplied by fifteen. He tried to do the sum in his head, the thousands first, then the tens. He lost count, and when he opened his eyes it was morning.

He left the house early. He knew what he had to do. A few minutes later, he arrived at the post office on Place des Abbesses. He went in, and made for the *poste restante* counter. Holding out his identity card, he said:

"Lomel. Etienne Lomel."

He did not suppose that, if there were a letter for his wife, it would be handed over to him. Still, the clerk had taken the letters from the pigeonhole marked *L,* and was looking through them, standing at the counter. He watched her hands as they turned over a pile of envelopes of all shapes and colors.

"Did you say Etienne?"

She had stopped at a white envelope, and was leaning forward to examine his identity card.

"No, it's not for you."

Still, there was a letter addressed to Lomel, to Madame Louise Lomel. He had seen it, and tried to read the postmark. He was almost sure that it came from Bordeaux.

"Thank you."

"Not at all."

She watched him go, struck no doubt by the coincidence. She would almost certainly mention it to Louise. As it had started to rain again, he did not linger outside, but crossed the square and went into a café.

Louise had left the house earlier than on Saturday, and could not have stopped long on the way, for he saw her almost at once on Rue des Abbesses, walking toward the post office with rapid strides.

Today, she was happy, lingering in there, reading and re-reading her letter.

When she came out, she was still holding it in her hand. She opened her handbag and slipped it in.

She had got back her poise and vivacity. He did not follow her. There was no point to it now.

There was a *cassoulet* for his lunch, a dish they rarely had, and he believed he understood the reason for it, and almost smiled at the thought that she could not control her impatience. He ate some of it, and went out to vomit, not at the bar on Place Blanche, but in the toilet of a tobacconist's shop on Rue Fontaine.

All afternoon, as he made his rounds, he was trying to think who, among the people she knew, might be in Bordeaux.

Could it be a commercial traveler like himself? Except for casual customers who came in to buy a pencil or a writing pad, they were the only people she saw apart from himself.

He knew the names of some of them, representatives of the big firms, whom they had dealt with for years. There were a great many others, most of whom did not call more than once or twice a year.

She had not thrown the letter away. She had brought it

home, maybe because she wanted to read it just once more before destroying it. He even believed that, hidden away somewhere or other, there might be a whole bundle of such letters.

He went home to find her just as he had always known her, serene and placid. He slumped as he came in the door, assuming an air of intense weariness.

"Anything wrong?"

Something instinctively drove him to tell a lie.

"I had an attack—very much worse than the others."

"While you were with a customer?"

"No. In the street. Actually, it was on Place de la Bastille, not far from your sister's."

Trivau's pharmacy was on Rue de la Roquette, about a hundred yards from Rue de Lappe.

"Did you go there?"

She was alarmed. That was as he had intended.

"I would have, but I could hardly stand, let alone walk. I propped myself up against a wall. There were brothels on both sides, and tarts standing around outside. They thought I'd come for them. Several actually accosted me."

It was true that he had been near the Bastille, but nothing had occurred. He had mentioned tarts, because, as it happened, one had grabbed him by the arm that afternoon.

He had, moreover, gone past Trivau's dark little shop, on the opposite side of the road, and he had seen the shadowy figure of his brother-in-law, talking to a customer.

"It did occur to me that Trivau might be able to give me something to relieve the pain. But then, just because you and your sister have made up, it doesn't necessarily mean that we want to get mixed up with him again, does it?"

"So you didn't go into the shop?"

"No, in the end I went into a bar. I felt very sick, but I couldn't bring anything up. I must have looked ghastly, because everyone was staring at me. The owner actually offered to go and get a doctor."

He must watch himself. He was laying it on too thick.

"But it did ease up in the end?"

"Not for half an hour or so."

"But you finished your round?"

"I was all right afterward. Just tired. I'm still very tired."

"You'll have to go to bed after dinner."

"I think I'd better."

He had a great deal to think about that night, as he lay in bed listening to the noises in the street. He was, in a strange way, at once lighthearted and sad. He had not abandoned his plan. His decision was irrevocable. All the same, now that the critical moment was at hand, he was beginning to wonder whether he had chosen the best course.

"Good night, Etienne."

Starting as though he had been dozing, he put his arms around her and held her very close. He was not playacting. He genuinely longed to feel the warmth of her body, to establish contact with her again.

Was she, at that moment, thinking of the other man?

"Don't you think you ought to be resting?" she protested, gently.

"Yes, you're right."

He had forgotten that he should be feeling unwell, that he was supposed to have had an attack.

"Good night, Louise."

He fell asleep at last, and next morning, when he awoke, it was still raining.

"You'd better take your umbrella, for the shopping."

"I won't be going today. We've got all we need in the house. I'll just have to telephone the butcher."

All the same, he went to Rue des Abbesses, where he found the same clerk on duty at the *poste restante* counter. She recognized him, and said, as he held out his identity card:

"Still nothing for you."

As she had just finished sorting the mail, he left it at that.

Mashed potatoes, since it was Tuesday. Finger rammed down throat. Hard-boiled eggs, and a glass of beer.

He telephoned Boulevard de Clichy several times because it was his habit, and he must at all costs avoid arousing suspicion. He walked almost his entire round, from Place de la République to Place de la Bastille, where they had a fair number of working-class customers.

Louise must have known that there would be no letter that day. By next morning, the rain had stopped. Indeed, from the look of the sky, it might have been spring.

Would there be a letter for her today, he wondered?

He had to leave a few minutes earlier than usual, to be sure of getting to Place des Abbesses before she did. Once more, the girl at the poste restante desk recognized him, and shook her head, but he was politely insistent. Assuming a worried expression, he said:

"Do me a favor, and have another look, will you?"

She must have thought that he was in love, and that his girl had let him down. It was all the same to him. As though she felt sorry for him, she took the pile of letters from the pigeonhole marked *L,* and thumbed through them. He leaned forward to peer at them.

There was one for Louise, and, from the postmark, he could see that it came from Toulouse.

Bordeaux . . . Toulouse . . . Louise's correspondent was farther from Paris now, not nearer, but the knowledge gave
Etienne no satisfaction. Indeed, it made him sick at heart, for
now all he wanted was to get it over with as quickly as possible. If it was one of the travelers who toured the whole
country, he might have to wait weeks, or even months.

He went back to the bistro across the road. Twenty minutes
later, Louise appeared, wearing a dress with a white collar
under her coat. She was inside for about the same length of
time as before, and came out with her letter in her hand.

She was on her way to the butcher's, and he was waiting
for her to go in, so that he could slip away. He finished his
glass of white wine diluted with Vichy water, and was just
paying for it, when a familiar figure appeared in the doorway.

It was Arthur Leduc, coatless, with his hat pushed to the
back of his head.

"Etienne!" he exclaimed, unable to conceal his surprise.
"What are you doing here?"

Etienne, at a loss, waved toward his empty glass. "You
see . . . I . . ."

He was afraid that Arthur might turn around and see
Louise, who was not yet out of sight.

"Have you many customers around here?"

"A few."

"What will you have?"

The proprietor, stretching out a hand across the bar, said,
as though he knew him well:

"Good morning, Monsieur Arthur. How are you?"

Etienne dared not refuse the glass of Pouilly. It was Wednesday. Next evening, the Leducs would be dining and playing
cards with them on Boulevard de Clichy.

"How's Louise?"

"Very well."

"And you?" He said this with real concern.

"Fine."

"You're not still feeling under the weather?"

"A bit. I'll get over it."

There was no time for reflection. He had to think quickly. He said, "Look here, Arthur," feeling so thoroughly uncomfortable that he had no need to put on an act. He spoke almost in a whisper; the proprietor was within earshot, wiping off the tables.

"I'd be glad if you would say nothing to my wife about meeting me here."

Arthur was staggered. For appearances' sake, he was doing his best not to show it, but it was obvious all the same.

Averting his eyes, Etienne went on:

"I'm supposed to be in the Third Arrondissement. I'd rather you didn't mention seeing me this morning, even to Mariette."

What must Leduc be thinking? That he had a girl friend? That was what he wanted him to believe.

"I had to see someone. You understand, don't you?"

"My lips are sealed, old man."

Still obviously dazed, he made an attempt to shrug it off with a jest:

"Blonde or brunette?"

"Blonde."

"Pretty?"

"One always thinks they're pretty, surely?"

His friend responded with a hearty slap on the back, but his heart was not in it.

"Good for you!"

He did not sound as though he meant it.

"You promise?"

"What d'you take me for?"

"Not a word, even to your wife?"

"Do you think Mariette has to be told everything I do?"

Nevertheless, Etienne was sick with anxiety all the rest of the day.

3

On Thursday morning, there was a letter. Fortunately, the regular clerk was off duty, or she would probably just have shaken her head to show that there was nothing for him, and he would not have dared, this time, to urge her to take another look.

It had occurred to him that his visits to the post office would look more genuine if he were to address letters to himself occasionally, but he could not take the risk of their being seen by Louise.

As before, he peered at the letter, trying to decipher the postmark, and said insistently:

"Are you sure it's not for me?"

The clerk, with a suspicious look, hastily thrust the bundle back into its pigeonhole. He had not been able to read the name of the town. This worried him. He felt lost, for now he could not tell whether the man—whoever he might be—was coming nearer or traveling farther afield.

Still, there was one thing to be thankful for. This morning, because of his meeting with Arthur on the previous day, he observed Louise as she came in sight, even more closely than before, and there was no change in her. She did not once look back over her shoulder, which seemed to indicate that, even if Leduc had spoken to Mariette, she had not telephoned Louise to put her on her guard.

Possibly, Arthur had not said anything. The more Etienne thought about it, the more confident he felt that he could be trusted to keep a secret. He would have liked to know him better, to make a real friend of him. At heart, he was sure, Arthur was a diffident, possibly an unhappy man.

What did he really know of the Leducs? In the past fifteen years, seeing Mariette and Arthur once a week, he had learned nothing about their private life. What, for instance, was the bond that united them? The fact that they were husband and wife meant nothing. Now, he would probably never find out anything more. It was too late.

There must have been something different about this letter, for Louise was agitated when she came out of the post office. She was still tense when he got home at midday, though she did her best to seem at ease.

It was not grief or despair that she felt, as on the day when no letter had come. Rather, it seemed that she was in the grip of some urgent problem, and several times, when their eyes met, she looked away.

Early in the afternoon, he had an attack. It surprised him, for they had both eaten the same things for lunch. Nevertheless, he recognized the symptoms, burning sensations in the throat, spasms in the chest, and, for almost half an hour, a pulse rate of 55.

Had she perhaps decided to poison the coffee on days when there was no dish made especially for him? She drank coffee as well. It would not have been easy for her to put the poison in his cup without his noticing. Admittedly, he had not been watching her. From now on, he must be careful to observe her every gesture, for he couldn't possibly throw up everything he ate or drank at home.

Life was getting more and more complicated, but he was keeping his end up. Even the attack during which he took refuge in a brasserie, where no one paid the slightest attention to him, had not broken his spirit. But he wanted it over and done with, and the sooner the better.

Almost immediately after this, there was another incident. He telephoned Boulevard de Clichy and heard, not his wife's voice, but that of Monsieur Charles.

"Isn't my wife in?"

"No, monsieur."

"Has she been out long?"

"Not more than ten minutes or so."

"Do you know where she's gone?"

"No, monsieur."

He was beginning to detest Monsieur Charles, for no particular reason, though he was sure that the feeling was mutual, or, rather, that the stockman had never regarded him with anything but contempt.

A quarter of an hour later, he rang again, and Louise answered. She had been told of his earlier call.

"Is that you? Sorry I missed you just now. I'd completely forgotten that today was Thursday, and I didn't have anything to serve the Leducs. I had to dash out to Rue Lepic and buy some fish."

It was a plausible excuse. She was at least as quick-witted as he was. They hardly ever had fish for the Leducs, but, if she had been giving them meat, she would have had no excuse

148

for going out, as she could always give the butcher her order over the telephone. He concluded that, for one reason or another, she had been to the post office again.

"Are you all right?" she asked.

"I've had an attack."

"A bad one?"

"Yes, but I'm feeling better now."

"Aren't you coming home?"

"I've got two more calls to make."

She must have been expecting a second letter by the afternoon post. Had it come?

He cursed himself for not having kept a closer watch on her. On the other hand, he could not stand guard from morning till night on Place Blanche without giving himself away; he had to get through his rounds.

What he must do now was to get back on the trail as soon as possible.

He got home a quarter of an hour before the Leducs arrived. There was indeed fish in the oven—sole au gratin—and Louise herself was supervising the cooking. She was a very good cook. The heat of the stove had given her a high color. Being in a rush, she scarcely noticed him, so that he could not judge her state of mind.

It was he who went to the door to answer the bell, and Arthur, coming in behind his wife, took the opportunity to give him a reassuring wink, which was decent of him.

"Where's the boss?"

"She's busy in the kitchen."

They took off their things. As he handed around the drinks, it seemed to him that Mariette's eyes were unusually bright, and her cheeks very pink. It struck him that she looked younger.

When Louise came in to join them, he did not catch any exchange of glances between her and Mariette, but, right at the start of the meal, as though she could not contain herself any longer, Mariette said to her husband:

"Do you mind if I tell them?"

Arthur looked at her as though she were a little girl.

"Why should I? You'll tell them anyway."

"Please, you two, don't make fun of me. I'm almost ashamed of having it happen at my age. Just think of it, I'm pregnant!"

She laughed, and it would not have taken much to make her weep for joy. As for Arthur, he was looking serious, even as he smiled. Etienne knew that, for twenty years, they had both wanted a child.

Mariette's hopes had been raised at least a dozen times before. Each time, she had trembled with happiness, and each time, after two or three months, it had ended in a miscarriage. They had lost count of the times she had been in the hospital, and, a few years back, she had almost died.

"What do you say to that? An old woman like me! I haven't even dared tell my girls at the shop. If ever I take the baby out for a walk, everyone will think I'm its grandmother."

Etienne was not the only one to see that Louise was not taking it in. She smiled politely, but her mind was elsewhere. Mariette noticed it, too, and was disconcerted.

"I light a candle to the Virgin, every morning!" she went on.

The Leducs were not churchgoers as a rule, but Louise, engrossed in her own problems, gave no sign of having heard, and later, while they were playing *belote,* she made several careless slips. By way of apology, she said:

"Please don't be cross with me, my dears. It's just that I've had the most appalling neuralgia ever since lunch."

"Why didn't you tell me?" Etienne asked.

"It's nothing compared to what you've been through."

He had never known her to be ill. She had never even had a cold or bronchitis, which was remarkable, considering that both her parents had died of tuberculosis.

The Leducs insisted on leaving earlier than usual. This time, it was Etienne who pressed Arthur's hand with especial warmth, though he was not quite sure whether it was to thank him for his discretion, or because of their hopes of having a child.

"Have you taken anything for it?" he asked his wife, when they were alone.

"I had two pills after lunch. I'll take two more now."

She had seemed preoccupied after getting the first letter that morning. Had she had further worrying news since then?

He slept badly, troubled by confused dreams, which were only remotely connected with his real problems. He walked endlessly through a maze of unfamiliar streets, whose buildings were all of gray stone, as in a medieval town. He was on his way somewhere. He must get there at all costs. It was a matter of life and death.

He had lost the slip of paper with the address, and there was no one to direct him. The streets were empty, as were the houses.

He knew that there was very little time, and began to run. When at last he came to a public square, where a great crowd was assembled as for a political meeting, people turned around to look at him reproachfully, and put a finger to their lips.

He was breaking some rule, but what had he done wrong? He wished he knew, because the last thing he wanted was to cause offense. They were all looking at something, and he craned his neck, trying to see over their heads. Suddenly the crowd parted, leaving a clear path in front of him, and he saw, at the end of it, an enormous tomb.

They were all waiting to see what he would do. As he made no move, a woman in mourning, who looked like old Madame Coin, touched him on the shoulder, urging him forward.

He had other, equally oppressive dreams. He was wandering about all night. At one point, awakened by a party of four who had been to a cabaret and were arguing at the top of their voices with a taxi driver at the corner of Place Blanche, he reminded himself that next morning he must be sure to get rid of the scribbled notes hidden in the Fabre book.

They were out of date. He was past that stage. The new maid might dislodge the sheet of paper while dusting, or Louise herself might happen to open the book.

He got up feeling tired. His wife's face was almost as drawn as his own. He got to Place des Abbesses before she did, and went to the *poste restante* counter. The girl who knew him by sight was back on duty.

"I'll bet there's a letter for me today!" he exclaimed jocularly.

"I'll bet there isn't."

She glanced through the bundle.

"Let me look."

He could not get a close view of the letters, but he was able to catch a glimpse of his wife's name on a telegram.

"Are you sure that isn't for me?"

"Certain."

"It looks like my name."

"I'm very sorry, but it's not for you."

All morning, he was almost as excited as Louise appeared to be when, a little later, she left the post office. He stayed as close as he dared to Place Blanche, shifting his ground twenty times over, to avoid being noticed. After doing her shopping, his wife went indoors and stayed there.

It would not be long now, he knew, because as he went through the shop, a few minutes after midday, when she was already upstairs, he glanced toward the cashier's desk and, in one of the pigeonholes behind her stool, saw a railway timetable that was not usually kept there.

She scarcely noticed him, too deeply immersed in her own thoughts to remember to keep an eye on him. For his part, he forgot to watch her while she poured out the coffee. He did not want to drink it, but dared not refuse the cup she held out to him, and had therefore to go out and vomit afterward, for he could not afford to run the smallest risk.

He made no calls that day, and was ready with a plausible excuse, in case she asked questions; but she did not. He drank three small glasses of brandy, which was unusual for him, because he could not stand guard on the sidewalk the whole time, and people were drinking all around him.

He telephoned at three and five o'clock. At five, the line was busy. He stayed in the telephone booth, and wasted six minutes or more trying to get his number. Business calls at the shop were usually kept short.

Seeing the railway timetable in the shop at lunchtime had given him an idea. He would look up the trains from Toulouse. The express, he found, got into Paris at 4:45. This, he thought, explained everything.

Someone must have put a call through to Louise from the station, or from a nearby café. He did not go home until six, and when he did get in, he announced casually, as though he were resigned to it, that he had had another attack.

She did not seem surprised. She was much more vivacious than she had been that morning or the night before. Her manner was almost playful, though perhaps a little feverish. The brilliance of her eyes reminded him of Mariette making plans for her baby.

She, too, was anticipating a great event, and she was on tenterhooks. When Emma had cleared the table, Louise suggested that they go to a movie. This was unusual for her, especially on a Friday.

She could not bear to be shut up alone with him all evening. He almost said no, out of spite, to get a little of his own back, but, on reflection, it seemed best to give in to her. She went to freshen up, and he watched her as she applied a dab of perfume behind the ears.

They went to a movie house on Boulevard Rochechouart, and, all the way through the film, Etienne was on his guard. It was just possible that she had suggested this outing in order to see someone, if only in the distance. He scrutinized the faces of the passers-by, and, in the movie house, took a good look at the people closest to them, turning around more than once to do so.

When they were almost at their door, it was she, once again, who took the initiative.

"What about having a drink at the Cyrano?"

It was just opposite, on the corner of Rue Lepic. The terrace was used the whole year round, though in cold weather it was enclosed in glass and heated by braziers. The people inside were strung out like exhibits in a glass case, as they sat looking at the illuminations on Place Blanche, and the blurred outlines of the passers-by.

They had come here hundreds of times at night, after a show or a stroll through the neighborhood. They knew most of the local prostitutes by sight. The old flower woman, who was always drunk on red wine, and never tired of talking about her splendid past as a kept woman, tonight merely smiled as they went by, and left them in peace.

Louise did not appear to be searching for anyone in the crowd, and he saw no one looking with special interest at her.

When they got home, he was tempted to make love to her, knowing that she would not dare to refuse. With her lover now so close, would it not be torture for her?

He did not make love to her, whether because he did not have the courage, or because he pitied her, or both, he could not say. She kissed him as always. They spoke the customary words, including, after the usual pause: "Are you asleep?"

In the morning, she caught herself singing in the bathroom, and, seeing his look of surprise, exclaimed, by way of excuse:

"Look at the sun shining. It's glorious!"

She was right. It was heart-warming to see the golden light playing on the few yellow leaves still left on the branches, which trembled in the breeze, making the sun itself seem to shimmer.

After breakfast, she said:

"Where are you going this morning?"

"I think I'll take advantage of the weather, and do the Fourteenth Arrondissement."

Of all his rounds, this was the farthest from home. They did not have many customers in the area, but those they had were spread out, which meant a good deal of walking for him. As a rule, when he did this round, he had lunch out.

She did not ask him whether he would be home for lunch that day, and did not turn around when he opened the door of the bedroom to say good-by.

She was dressing. She had on her panties and brassière, with a broad band of naked flesh between, and was bending forward, in a familiar attitude, to fasten her garters.

He had made up his mind that once he was out of the house he would get rid of his case, which had been such a nuisance the day before.

He deposited it at the bar on Place Blanche, and lingered there, waiting.

When Louise came out at about a quarter past nine, she was not dressed for shopping, but was wearing her newest coat, which, like most of her clothes, was nipped in at the waist and full over the hips. Her hat, which he had only seen her wear once before, had white trimmings, and a little tulle veil over the eyes.

She was not carrying her shopping bag. She was walking more briskly than she had done on her way to Rue Lepic, and her high heels rapped out a cheerful rhythm on the sidewalk.

For days on end he had lived for this moment, yet, as he watched her turning the corner of the square onto Rue Fontaine, he was seized with panic—so much so that, had it been possible, he would have begged for a reprieve.

He waited until she was some way ahead of him, then followed, keeping well on the inside of the sidewalk, so that, if she should look back, he could take cover in the nearest doorway. At this hour, through the open doors of the night clubs, cleaners could be seen at work, sweeping up paper streamers and pellets of cotton wool. Most of the entrances were plastered with photographs of more or less naked women. He noticed an ash-blonde girl coming out of a hotel, very young, in evening dress, hugging a fur stole around her shoulders. Her make-up was streaky, her long, trailing dress dusty at the hem, and she was looking at the bustling crowds in the street as though she felt sick at heart.

At the corner of Rue Notre-Dame-de-Lorette, he lost sight of Louise, quickened his pace almost to a run, peered anxiously down the side streets, and saw her at last on the sidewalk of the almost deserted Rue la Rochefoucauld, where the only touch of color was the sunlit flag over the police headquarters.

He dared not go farther. He wondered whether he ought to hail a taxi, so as to be able to follow her without being seen. He might have done so, had he not, just then, seen her turn unhesitatingly into a café restaurant on the corner of Rue la Bruyère. They had dined there together once or twice.

He remembered that the walls inside were painted yellow, a creamy yellow, set off by red checkered curtains. In the front room, where the bar was, there were only three tables, and these were always occupied at lunchtime by regular customers, who were on familiar terms with the owner.

The back room was not much bigger, and he recalled the green plants on the window sills, which had put him in mind of a provincial dining room.

It was not the kind of place one would choose for a quick drink. At this hour, it was probably empty. The sun was shining full on it, flickering on the walls inside through the chinks in the curtains. In spite of the need for caution, he ventured a few paces into the street, and could see that the door was open. A little later the proprietor, in his shirt sleeves, emerged, carrying a light-colored cloth, which he shook out on the sidewalk.

A dog, a small chocolate-colored dog, came out of the café, and ambled lazily along the street, sniffing at the buildings. Etienne dared not venture farther down the road. For one thing, he could not be certain that Louise was in the back room, and for another, he was uncomfortably aware that there was a policeman on duty outside the headquarters.

Most people had their windows open, and he could see the women at their housework. In one window, there was a canary hopping around in a cage, and a little girl leaning on the sill, watching it, with her chin resting on her folded arms.

There were no bedrooms attached to the restaurant, he was sure. It was not a hotel. He did not take comfort in the fact. For some reason, it irritated him.

He was expecting Louise to come out any minute now with her companion. He remembered how she used to burst into the room on Rue Lepic, sometimes stripping off her dress before she had even kissed him. There had been sunshine then, too. He recalled her body as her dark clothes dropped in a heap to the floor, and her breasts, of which she had always been proud, as she came toward him.

He was now standing in the entrance to a building where he could hide when they left the restaurant. The entrance was cool, there was a deserted courtyard at the back, and the concierge was not at her post.

He remembered that the specialty of the restaurant was tripe *à la mode de Caen*. They had gone back there several times, always in the summer for some reason or other. The proprietor's name was Oscar. He came from Normandy, and the sweetish smell of Calvados pervaded the bar.

Were they just sitting there, in the back room, sipping their drinks and gossiping?

He was growing tired of waiting. He thought he could see the policeman on duty peering suspiciously at him.

He walked a little way up the street, then back.

Hardly a day went by when he did not see a couple, alone in the back room of a bar, side by side on a bench, talking in lowered voices, hand in hand, as though the rest of the world did not exist. He had often looked at them with envy.

It had never been like that with Louise. He could not recall having once met her in a café; they had never had those long, whispered conversations.

The thought disturbed and vexed him. He had not been prepared for this.

Louise and her lover had been parted for a long time, possibly for weeks, certainly for days, and there they were, sitting in the little restaurant, gazing into each other's eyes.

The proprietor, his work done, was in the doorway, with his hands in the pockets of his white overall. He called back the dog, which had wandered off, and then just stood there, with an air of vacant contentment, blinking at the sun.

After ten minutes or so, he must have heard someone calling, for he turned around, and went inside. Possibly, Etienne thought, his wife and her companion were even now paying the bill, and would, at last, be coming out.

After a little while, Oscar reappeared, still with the same air of contentment. There was no one else. He had probably gone in to refill their glasses.

A voice asking for a match made Etienne start. He had not noticed anyone coming toward him. He was so shaken that he felt mechanically in his pockets for matches, before stammering out:

"I'm sorry. I don't smoke."

The strain of waiting was making him feel ill, almost as though he were having an attack. He dared not leave his post to get a glass of mineral water at the tobacconist's on the corner. In his heavy overcoat, he found the heat oppressive.

They were in there close to an hour; to be precise, fifty-five minutes. A truck had drawn up outside the restaurant, crates of liquor had been unloaded, and the engine was just starting up, when the couple emerged, at long last.

At once, Louise did what he had so often seen Mariette do. She took her companion's arm and clung to it, and, as they walked slowly up the street, she leaned toward the man, her shoulder pressing against his.

159

Etienne had stepped back under the archway. He could not risk being seen as they came toward him. They were walking on the opposite side of the street, and soon he could hear the murmur of their voices, in spite of the noisy buses on Rue Fontaine. Louise was speaking, but he could not make out what she was saying. They walked on a few yards, and as they drew level with him, he was able, by bending his head, to see them in profile, still in the same attitude. Louise was behaving like a young girl in love for the first time.

They did not laugh or raise their voices; their faces were grave, and they seemed to be savoring this moment in their lives. Etienne could not see the man's face clearly, because Louise's hat was in the way.

When they stopped, just short of the corner of Rue Notre-Dame-de-Lorette, they turned to face each other, standing motionless as they looked into each other's eyes, then came together in a long kiss. It was Louise who broke away at last. She walked on abruptly, turning back once to wave a gloved hand at the man, who stood watching her go.

She quickened her pace, and was soon out of Etienne's sight, but her companion was still gazing after her. She must have turned around again, because Etienne saw him wave.

Soon her young man, too, lost sight of her. Moving with easy grace, he boarded a bus going in the direction of Montparnasse.

Etienne had recognized him. He was Roger Cornu, son of Monsieur Théo, the printer. In the days when the Cornus lived near the shop, Madame Cornu used sometimes to call for her husband at six o'clock on a summer evening, pushing a baby carriage. Later, she came hand in hand with her small son, Roger, who would tear around the shop, in spite of his mother's efforts to keep him quiet.

That had been in Guillaume's time. Louise was already a grown woman, recently married.

Etienne turned onto Rue Fontaine, but could not make up his mind whether to head for Place Blanche or to go toward the center of town. What did it matter, anyway?

According to his reckoning, Roger must be about twenty-six years old. He himself had been only twenty-four when it all started.

The boy did not look like his father. He was taller, broad-shouldered, with dark hair growing low on his forehead, and blue eyes under bushy brows.

What made Etienne think of Arthur just then? If he had known where he was to be found, he might have gone to him. Not to take him into his confidence—it was too late for that—but just to get away from the streets, where he was utterly alone, a tiny island in a sea of people.

Without any definite plan in mind, he found himself back in the quiet of Rue la Rochefoucauld, and walking toward the little café with the yellow paint on the walls.

He was sure that the proprietor would not recognize him after all this time. They had never been regular customers.

Catching sight of his reflection in the window of a pork butcher's, he thought he looked like a poor specimen. He stood there uncertainly, then, at last, turned and went into the bar, where he laid his hands on the cool metal counter, and stared hungrily at the red bench in the back room.

The dog was sniffing at the cuffs of his trousers. The proprietor, who was busy crushing ice, wiped his hands, took one look at him, and said:

"Not feeling too good?"

He deliberately avoided looking at himself in the mirror.

4

But for the words of the concierge, things might have taken a different course. Those words had never been out of his mind, and had become an obsession during his three days in bed, after that Thursday when Louise had shut herself up in their room with Mariette, and they had stayed there, whispering, for ages. His very decision to go on living was probably owing to the picture conjured up by the words he had overheard long ago, through the open window.

"When they lifted him into the coffin, he weighed no more than a child of ten."

He could not shut out the image of Guillaume Gatin, with his hat on his head, his light-fawn coat, and his mustache, dwarfed and wizened, until he was no taller and no heavier than a ten-year-old boy. For he always pictured Guillaume shrunken in bone as well as flesh.

It was not too late to throw in the sponge, and he was tempted to do so. He regretted going into the little restaurant, where he was now standing, with his eyes focused on the bench. As for the proprietor, who had seen them and heard them, and who was now handing him a glass of Calvados, and telling him that if he took it in one gulp it would do him good, the very sight of him made Etienne sick.

"What do I owe you?"

"Won't you stop and rest for a minute or two?"

He was tempted to stay.

"Is it heart trouble?"

To avoid discussion, he nodded. He had better leave at once. Later, he might not have the strength.

How much simpler it would be to let things take their course! He was getting used to his attacks. They no longer distressed him deeply, as they had done at first, and, it must be admitted, they were less painful. How many more would there be?

After taking to his bed for good, Guillaume had lingered on for another three months. There would be less time for Etienne. Louise could never feel safe with him. She would have to give him larger or more frequent doses. Maybe, by this time, she had decided to get it over with once and for all?

He had begun to lose weight. He would lose more, and soon his legs would refuse to carry him upstairs. Once he was up there, the days would pass like those three days that he had already spent in bed. He would feel the bristles sprouting on his chin, and the sweat trickling down his body, and he would grow weaker and weaker, in mind as well as in body. Dreams and reality would melt into one another, until at last the time came for his heart to stop beating altogether.

He was not outraged. He had always known that, sooner or later, something terrible would happen; it was, he felt, no more than he deserved. He had kept silent that other time, knowing all the facts, and, even though some things had never been put into words, he was just as guilty as Louise.

In answering "yes" when a certain question was put to him, he had pronounced Guillaume's death sentence.

The years during which they had been together were merely a breathing space. They had lived accordingly, waiting, waiting, year after year, and in those years he had felt the need, an increasingly agonizing need, to lose himself in Louise, to become one with her, because it was for this that the thing had been done; it was their only excuse, if any excuse were admissible.

And it was for this same reason that she, as much as he, had fiercely warded off any intrusion into their lives by other people.

They had been recluses, entrenching themselves deeper and deeper in their isolation. They had shrunk into themselves, and their narrow world was contained within their apartment, their bedroom, their bed, as they fought desperately to attain the impossible, to become totally one, to a degree forbidden in the union of male and female.

He had made up his mind to go on living. He did not want to go back on his decision. He had also made up his mind to keep Louise for himself.

It was not that he wanted to escape punishment, only to share it with her as they had always shared everything. The outcome might well be more appalling than if he gave up fighting for his life.

He would not go back to Boulevard de Clichy for lunch, because he knew that he could not look his wife in the face without betraying himself. If he were to set foot in the building and go upstairs to their apartment, he would never leave it again.

He walked along the street, following, almost step by step, the route that those two had taken, a short time before. And, like Roger Cornu, he boarded a bus going toward Montparnasse.

He had announced his intention of making calls in the Fourteenth Arrondissement. Had Louise been struck by the coincidence, he wondered? Had she believed that he had said it deliberately? It so happened that the offices of the firm for which Roger worked were on Avenue du Parc Montsouris, behind the Lion de Belfort.

Roger, no doubt, was on his way there now with a quarter of an hour's start. Etienne got off the bus at the first stop, and went into a café to telephone.

It was essential to make this call before Monsieur Théo's son arrived at his office. His firm, a very large concern, occupied the whole building. The success or failure of his plan was in the hands of the switchboard operator.

"I don't suppose Monsieur Cornu happens to be in his office?"

"One moment, please."

She did not plug in to an extension, which was a promising sign, but seemed to be consulting one of the other operators.

"No. But he's expected in, any minute."

"Would you please give me his private address?"

This was the critical moment. As it happened, she saw no harm in his request, and again turned to her colleague for information.

"It is the Hôtel de Quimper, isn't it, Jeannette?"

"Yes, at the corner of Rue Dareau."

The girl repeated:

"Hôtel de Quimper, at the corner of Rue Dareau. Do you wish to leave a message?"

"There wouldn't be any point. I'm not staying in Paris. If I don't find him at his place, I'll leave a note for him."

If she should mention the incident to Roger, it was very unlikely that he would think of connecting it with Etienne. He walked as far as the next stop, and took the bus all the way to Place d'Alésia. One of his customers had a shop just across the square.

He stopped in, wishing that he had not left his sample case at Place Blanche. He took an order all the same, and the customer didn't seem to notice anything amiss.

He now knew that it was in December that the affair between his wife and the Cornu boy had started. They had decided to buy a new printing press, and one evening she had said:

"Guess who called today from the Printers' Supply Company."

Needless to say, he had not been able to guess.

"Roger, Monsieur Théo's son."

The last time he had seen the boy, one day in the shop, he had been sixteen or seventeen years old, and had just started a course at the School of Arts and Crafts. He was thin and gangling in those days, with the beginnings of a mustache. He had gone in to see his father in the glass-walled printing office, and later Monsieur Théo had told them that he was considered a brilliant student, and had been awarded a scholarship.

In December, Louise had said:

"He has a very responsible job. It felt odd, somehow, to be discussing business with him. After all, I've known him since he was a child. He's an engineer, and they're always sending

166

him up and down the country to install their machinery. He's as shy as ever, though. He said he'd call again tomorrow."

No doubt he had called several times, though Etienne had not run into him, and his wife had not mentioned him again.

It was' midday. Louise would be at the cashier's desk on Boulevard de Clichy, wondering whether he would be home for lunch. When she had got back, had she changed her dress?

Should he telephone the shop? He was of two minds about it, then decided that he would. At the sound of her voice, he almost hung up without speaking.

But he did manage to stammer:

"Is that you?"

"Where are you?"

"I've just left Dambois."

"Will you be out for lunch?"

This decided him, or, rather, it confirmed his decision.

"Yes."

"Are you all right?"

"Yes."

"No more attacks?"

He said no, though possibly he should have said yes. He was incapable of thinking clearly. He did not even try. He was like an automaton.

The essential thing was to complete the task he had set himself as quickly as possible, while he was still keyed up. As it was lunchtime, he went into a restaurant. There were snails on the menu, and he had a dozen, with a half bottle of wine, as he watched the people going by in the street. Someone at the next table ordered tripe, and, because of the restaurant on Rue la Rouchefoucauld where he had eaten tripe with Louise, he ordered it, too.

He was in no hurry. He did not have to see a lot of customers. It was of no importance now. He would not be called upon to give any account of himself.

His plan was to call on a customer on Avenue du Parc Montsouris, which would take him past the offices of the Printers' Supply Company.

There were no showrooms or display windows in the building, just a highly polished door, with an imposing bronze plate, and dozens of offices, three floors of them, where the employees, some wearing green eyeshades, could be seen at work near the windows.

The Hôtel de Quimper was not far away, on the opposite side of the avenue, near the railway overpass on Rue Dareau. It had only two floors. The proprietor and his wife could be seen having their meal at a round table in the room to the left of the entrance. The place had the look of a country inn.

"I don't suppose Monsieur Cornu is in, by any chance?"

"He's never in at this time. He'd have to be sick."

"Can you tell me when he'll be back?"

"Not before nine or ten at night."

His appearance, it seemed, inspired confidence.

"If you want him urgently, you can find him at his office."

"I know."

"Isn't he there, then?"

"Not at the moment."

"It's true, he's not very often there, but you'll find him most evenings having dinner at Titin's, on Place d'Alésia."

During lunch, Etienne had noticed Titin's on the opposite side of the square.

"Thank you."

"You're welcome."

He walked for miles. He called on four or five customers and talked to them rationally, while they discussed business matters, unaware of anything unusual about him. And all the time, his mind was full of Louise and himself.

In all probability, they had a good few years ahead of them in the apartment linked to the shop by the iron staircase, and on the surface life would go on exactly as before.

That other time, he had asked Louise no questions. Would she ask questions now?

What good would it do? There would be no need to say anything. He would just arrive home, and she would understand.

Every Thursday, the Leducs would come in for dinner and a game of *belote,* as they had always done. He would not take Arthur into his confidence, either. Mariette, most probably, would miscarry. Every morning, Monsieur Charles would raise the shutters in front of the shop, and Monsieur Théo, in his glass cage, would put on his gray overall in his usual deliberate manner.

He was sorry for Monsieur Théo. In the street, his shrunken body lost in his black overcoat, he had looked like a heart case to Etienne; it was to be feared that he might not recover from the shock.

There was nothing he could do about it. It was too late. He knew that his time was running out. He was reminded of it by one electric clock after another, every time he came to a busy crossroads.

He had located a gunsmith that morning on Boulevard Denfert-Rochereau.

He waited until five o'clock to go in, and only then remembered that, at five o'clock on the previous day, Roger had telephoned Louise from the station, or somewhere nearby.

It crossed his mind that possibly everything was already out of his hands, that in the morning they had decided to run off together, that Louise had gone home only to pack her things, and that he would be returning to an empty house.

On reflection, however, he thought it unlikely. Roger was quite capable of suggesting it, but she would never dream of abandoning the shop—she had far too much regard for her property.

"I want a revolver, please."

He spoke in his most casual voice.

"An automatic?"

"I don't know. A good revolver."

"A pocket model, or something larger?"

As far as he was concerned, it made no difference.

"To keep in the house."

He was shown a selection of revolvers of various sorts. He picked out one that seemed reasonably light and compact.

"Will one box of cartridges be enough?"

He said yes, paid, and left the shop with his parcel.

He did not go back for dinner to the restaurant where he had lunched, for fear of being seen by Roger, but walked some distance, until he found one that looked inviting, and went in. He put his parcel down on the bench beside him, and could feel it against his thigh. He took a long time over his meal.

It was dark outside. On Boulevard de Clichy, the shutters were down, and Louise, alone in the apartment, was probably growing anxious. Up to seven o'clock she could, in a pinch, persuade herself that he had been detained somewhere.

But after that? Would she think that he had succumbed to an attack in the street? Or would she realize that he knew everything?

She had suspected, at times, that he knew, especially that night when she had shut herself up with Mariette in the bedroom.

Maybe she had thought of telephoning Mariette to tell her of her fears, or just for the sake of hearing a familiar voice. In that case, would Arthur not be bound to tell his wife that he had seen Etienne at nine in the morning, in a bar on Place des Abbesses?

Thus forewarned, Louise would be frantic. She would look for some means of putting her lover on his guard. Had he told her where he was to be found at mealtimes?

To pass the time, after he had finished his dinner, he had two or three cups of coffee. He did not have any alcoholic drink. He was determined to keep his mind clear, determined, above all, that Louise should not see him, when he got home, otherwise than perfectly rational, and in full command of himself.

Toward eight o'clock, he went into the washroom with his parcel, unwrapped it, loaded the revolver with six cartridges, as the gunsmith had shown him, and slipped it into his pocket.

The feel of it as he went back into the dining room of the restaurant, and his multiple reflection in the mirrors, made him smile inwardly. He summoned the waiter.

It was the first time in years that he had been out in the streets alone at night, and it felt so strange to him that, from time to time, he turned his head, intending to make some remark to his wife.

He must not begin his vigil too early. He loitered in front of the lighted shopwindows, stopped to look at the posters and stills of a film outside a movie house, and listened to a couple of teen-age girls talking with great animation about an elderly man, who had apparently made one of them a proposition.

There were no curtains over the windows of Titin's on Place d'Alésia, and from across the square he recognized Roger, seated alone at a bare table near the bar, writing a letter.

A letter to Louise. He had not seen her that morning, but was no doubt counting on meeting her next day, at the same time, at the same place, in their little restaurant on Rue la Rochefoucauld. This was not a letter intended for the mail, to be collected from Place des Abbesses, like those he wrote when traveling. It was a letter that he meant to hand over to her himself, because there was so much to say, and because writing to her made him feel almost as though they were spending the evening together.

There was a policeman on duty at the corner, and Etienne thought it wiser not to loiter. He was not in the least afraid, but there was no point in taking unnecessary risks.

The rest was simple, so simple that there was nothing to it but the final gesture, the austere act, purged of false sentiment and grief.

As he made his way toward the corner of Rue Dareau and Avenue du Parc Montsouris, his mind was a blank; he was conscious of nothing but the coolness of the night, the humidity in the air, the resonance of his footsteps on the sidewalk, the voices of people going past.

The avenue was deserted. The lights, strung out like chains on either side, made it appear endless and timeless. It seemed to lead nowhere, looming out of the night at one end and melting into it at the other. In contrast, the lower half of Rue Dareau, with its single incandescent gas lamp near the railway overpass, was like a street in some provincial town.

A train went by. Etienne had not yet made up his mind where to stand. Through the curtains of the Hôtel de Quimper he could see the elderly proprietor and his wife. He was in an armchair reading aloud from the newspaper. She was sitting opposite, at the round table, peeling vegetables.

Had it perhaps been unwise to talk to them that afternoon?

They would remember him. But what description could they give of him? There were thousands of men of his age in Paris, all much alike in appearance and dress. As far as he knew, he had not a single distinguishing feature.

All the same, it worried him to see them there. He wondered how long it would be before they went to bed. He hoped that Roger would not come back too early.

At the same time, he was impatient to be on his way to Boulevard de Clichy and Louise. It would be all over by then. It would never happen again. He would know with absolute certainty that, for the rest of their lives, she belonged to him.

There was no moon, only a star or two, here and there. He had walked a long way, his legs were aching, and he was tempted to sit for a while on a bench under the trees. But, determined not to weaken, he stayed where he was.

A young couple went into the hotel. They were obviously newly married. They asked for their key, and then he heard their footsteps on the stairs. The footsteps stopped, a window on the second floor was flooded with light, then a hand appeared, and the curtains were drawn.

He could hear the sound of muffled music from a house close by, not radio music, but clumsy piano playing.

The playing stopped, and he heard footsteps coming toward him from Place d'Alésia. They stopped short of where he was standing, as a woman turned into the doorway of an apartment house.

At ten o'clock, the ground-floor lights of the hotel were turned out, leaving only a night light in the corridor. There was still no sign of Roger. This was his chance to move closer and wait, as he had meant to do all along, pressed close against the wall of the hotel, a few feet from the door.

He was so completely relaxed that he began debating with

himself whether, when he started for home presently, it would be quicker to go by bus or subway, bearing in mind that he must break his journey somewhere along the Seine, to get rid of the revolver.

All he felt now was a growing impatience; he reminded himself that he must keep a cool head.

When he heard the footsteps some way off—this time he could have sworn that they were the right footsteps—he plunged his hand into the pocket of his overcoat, where the revolver was, and his fingers tightened on the butt.

Some time earlier, he had heard a peal of bells, chiming the hour. It must be nearly half past ten.

The footsteps sounded regular and unhurried on the other side of the avenue, and, catching a glimpse of the man as he passed under a street lamp, Etienne knew that he had not been mistaken.

The moment had come. In two minutes, in one minute, it would be over. He forced himself to keep perfectly still, pressing so hard against the wall that his back ached, counting the footsteps. Being unsure of his aim, he had resolved to fire only at very close range.

He was convinced that Roger would not see him until the very last moment, when it would be too late. There was no need, as far as he was concerned, for Louise's lover to recognize him. It was not revenge that he was seeking. He felt no anger toward him, still less hatred.

He crossed the road and stepped onto the sidewalk.

Was it less dark than Etienne had imagined, or was the young man so familiar with his appearance that he could recognize him, even in shadow?

At any rate, he stopped dead, and gasped:

"Monsieur Lomel!"

He sounded stunned, but that was not all. He spoke with the deference of a child for a grownup, or the son of a workman for his father's boss.

His glance fell on Etienne's hand, still deep in his overcoat pocket. He realized at once what it meant, but made no move to escape, or to forestall Etienne.

He stood there, barely three feet away, waiting, resigned. Then, when nothing happened, when he saw that his adversary, too, was standing motionless, he said, in a hesitant undertone:

"Did you want to speak to me?"

Etienne's eyes were fixed on his face, a white patch in the surrounding darkness. He did not take his hand out of his pocket.

Then he, too, spoke, hearing his own voice with astonishment. He said, almost as though he were apologizing:

"No . . . I just happened to be passing. . . ."

He knew that he ought to start walking away, but found he could not move. Roger did not move, either, at first. It was as though he were giving him one last chance. There was a long pause, before Monsieur Théo's son turned to go indoors. Etienne thought that he had heard him say "Good night," before going into the hotel.

Had he replied?

He dragged himself away from the wall, and was crossing the road making for the trees, when he stumbled. Just at that moment, a car roared past and disappeared in the distance. It missed him by inches.

Half an hour later, several people who were still awake heard a noise like a gunshot, but it might have been a car backfiring, or a tire blowout.

Two or three people looked out of their windows, out of curiosity, but could see nothing.

It was not until very late, just before dawn, when the night was at its coldest, that a policeman found Etienne Lomel on a bench, with half his face shot away, and his fingers clenched around the gun.

Shadow Rock Farm
Lakeville, Connecticut
May 12, 1953